Hollywood Bilker

Leopold Borstinski

FEBRUARY 1960

1

"THANKS FOR TAKING the time to see me, Santo."

The Italian boss of Florida nodded his acknowledgment of Alex's words as they sipped their coffees in the back of one of the many casinos owned by the Sicilian in Miami-Dade county.

"Cuba was a terrible business for us all. I am only glad we got out with our lives."

"Santo, I don't think I ever saw Batista travel faster than his last minutes in power. That man knew the right time to flee."

"And he left the rest of us high and dry."

Now Alex nodded as he recalled the final two days in Havana, with his close friend and business associate, Meyer Lansky, as he attempted to salvage the gelt he had secreted around the city; they never trusted the banks.

"That was the past, Santo. Despite all that has happened, I am trying to focus on future opportunities."

"Spoken like a true businessman. How can I help?"

"I am hoping you'll make an introduction for me to Frank DeSimone out in Los Angeles."

"What's wrong with the Eastern Seaboard?"

"Nothing at all, I just want to get as far away from Cuba as possible, at least for a short while. Having spent so many years in the Vegas and Havana hotel complexes, I thought I might check out life in Hollywood. I've mixed with enough of the celebrities to know what they are like and I can see some opportunities for myself, subject to Frank's approval, of course."

"Alex, I will give you the introduction you seek with pleasure. You have proven yourself in the past and I wish you every success in your new enterprise."

The two men shook hands and Alex left the back room, knowing that by the time he contacted DeSimone, Santo would have put in a good word. What Alex failed to realize was that as a former syndicate member and the fella who still ran Las Vegas, his reputation was the only calling card he needed.

Perhaps his seven years spent in Cuba helping Meyer build a casino resort in paradise had left Alex jaded. In the four weeks since his return to the US, he had given no indication that he was a guy sitting on over two million bucks he had brought back to the country.

SARAH AND ALEX arrived at their Boyle Heights home less than a month later. They held hands as they walked up the drive, and Alex felt her fingers squeeze around his palm before he opened the front door.

"How long do you think we'll be here, Alex?"

"Beats the hell out of me, hon'. For now, I am thinking of finding a way to make some gelt and then we retire."

"I thought you'd saved sufficient money from Havana before we flew out?"

"You can never have enough cash. Besides, I'm too young to stop working, don't you think?"

"Without Meyer's accounts to look after, it looks like I will have time on my hands too."

"The first job we've both got to deal with is getting ourselves nested in this place."

They stood in the middle of the emptiness, which was their living room: bare floorboards, and no furniture. Sarah followed Alex as he sauntered to the rear of the house and opened up the doors onto their patio. The swimming pool was boarded over and the summerhouse looked uninviting.

Sarah let go of Alex's hand, dashed into the living room, and appeared on the balcony on the second floor. He waved at her and she laughed. They would do well here, he thought, as he considered what he was going to arrange with DeSimone.

FURNITURE AND SOFT furnishings changed their house into a home. Sarah had not wasted her years with Meyer as she took on the role of project manager for the transformation. She said what she wanted and when it needed to happen, and all the people working for her knew it too. She did not allow a single one to fail her.

Alex spent his time in the summerhouse, hiding from being asked his opinion on the colors of tables and chairs, but also to escape from the chill that hung in the air. They might have been away from Cuba for over a year, but he had still to acclimatize to the less than Caribbean temperatures.

Once Sarah declared the end of her project, Alex spent more time in the main building, although in that short while he had made the summerhouse his office.

"You can move your things into the den. I've decked it out especially for you."

"I like the fact that this has a different path to the entrance, Sarah."

"Is that to have discreet meetings without my seeing?"

"Having a detached place is nice. It means we can separate business from personal. And you are an essential part of the operation. Just because we are back in the US doesn't mean I intend to treat you the same way as when we were first married. My investments are your investments; we sink or swim together."

Sarah's shoulders sagged. "I had plans for the summerhouse: I thought we might turn it into a children's playroom."

"Children?"

"For when the grandkids visit."

Alex nodded, although he couldn't see David or Moishe schlepping over to the West Coast very often. Not that either of them had even met a woman, let alone produced an heir.

"Perhaps we could build a new spot for them."

"Or Alex, you could have an office a little further away from the pool."

He smiled. There was something fabulous about the idea of having a conversation about money laundering and then hopping into the water for a swim. Perhaps he could cope with a twenty-foot walk between the two activities and it would make Sarah happy too.

"Before we settle down too much, do you fancy taking a trip with me to Las Vegas? I have some business I want to sort out with Ezra and Massimo?"

"I'll stay here and leave you to speak to your men by yourself."

"That wasn't what I meant."

"I know, Alex. I'd rather spend some time enjoying the fresh nest I've built before I fly off."

THE NEXT DAY, Alex took one of the new jet planes over to Vegas and one of his lieutenant's drivers met him at the airport. Alex stood at the arrivals gate until a fella in a long black coat and a fedora walked up to him and asked if he had a light.

"Sure, Mac."

Alex proffered a match, and the guy nodded briefly and lit his cigar.

"You need a lift, Mac?"

"I'm waiting for someone, thanks."

"Are they coming from the Sands?"

Alex eyed him up and down and nodded.

"Then you've found your driver, Mr. Cohen."

"How do you know I'm this guy you mention?"

"You look the spit of your photo and you haven't denied being Alex Cohen."

He thought for a moment and decided this fella had made a good point.

"What's your name?"

"Tito Vestri. Follow me."

Tito grabbed Alex's case before he had a chance to protest and pounded out to the sidewalk where his limousine waited by a hydrant. A local cop stood nearby and appeared about to issue a ticket, but he took one look at Vestri and put away his notebook.

"GOOD TO SEE you, fellas, and thank you for making time for me with only a day's notice."

Alex was in his suite with Ezra Kohut and Massimo Sciarra for company. He lounged in an armchair, and the two others sat at either end of a matching leather couch. A bellboy had just left, having delivered coffee and some snacks that Ezra had ordered on his way up to Alex's room.

"We always have time for you, Alex. You should know that by now."

Alex smiled at Massimo for his kind words and his chest puffed out in response.

"How's business with you two?"

"Everything is good, Alex. Are you concerned about your end being short?"

"Not at all, Ezra. Should I be?"

"Oh no, not at all. It's just been a while since you've journeyed to visit us and I thought you might have a problem you wanted to discuss."

Alex's eyebrows took a few seconds to lower from their new high perch, but he relaxed as he took in Ezra's and Massimo's expressions.

"After our troubles in Havana, Sarah and I have spent some time putting ourselves back together. Now we have moved to Los Angeles, I thought the time was right for us to talk about the future. I've had enough of sitting in the Florida sun and want something to do."

Ezra looked at Massimo, who stared back. Neither wanted to say what they were thinking, but Alex knew there was an opinion to be uttered. He allowed silence to descend until one of them expressed their thoughts. Massimo was the first to break ranks.

"Do you want to take Vegas from us?"

Alex laughed.

"Quite the reverse. You have both been kind enough to provide me with my tithe, month in and month out, no matter what has been happening at home or away. While I am looking for my next opportunity, I also am thinking about separating my legitimate businesses from the rest. When I do, I want you two to be assured that I'll do the right thing by you in Vegas."

"You mean…"

"Yes, Ezra. In the near future, I will hand over control of my gaming interests to you and Massimo."

"I never thought I'd hear you talk of retiring, Alex."

"Soon, Massimo, but not just yet."

2

FRANK DESIMONE'S CASUAL dress caught Alex by surprise. He was expecting a suit and tie and was greeted by slacks and a plaid jumper. When he'd last lived on the West Coast, things were different, but that was before his Cuban escapade and America invaded Korea.

"Thank you for taking the time to see me, Frank."

"My pleasure, Alex. Apologies for my attire, but I have just hopped off the golf course as I was running late and did not have a chance to change."

"Not at all. That's a game I've never tried."

"Didn't they have any courses in Havana because they sure as hell do in Miami? Isn't that where you've been holed up this past year?"

"Pretty much, Frank. I guess I've never been bitten by the bug."

"You'll get there, Alex. In the meantime, how are you keeping yourself busy?"

"My interests in Las Vegas are served well by what you would describe as my capos and now I'm looking for a fresh opportunity in California."

"If there is anything specific you want to discuss, then I am all ears, but please don't expect me to throw you some crumbs from my plate."

Alex shuffled in his seat because he'd thought Santo would have primed Frank better. That said, Alex only wanted a little something to keep him afloat until the next big deal came across his lap, if it ever did.

"I was in the Sands Hotel a while back and met up with some old Hollywood friends: Frank Sinatra, Sammy Davis Jr., and Peter Langford. There were doing their schtick on stage when I was shooting through. Do you think you could sanction an import/export business focused on Burbank?"

"What are you looking to move?"

"A small amount of cocaine and marijuana."

"And girls?"

"If I can feed the party set, then it makes sense to fan the flames of entertainment while I am there. Would that be acceptable to you? I don't want to step on anybody's toes and if you've got that action covered, then I'll find something else."

"No disrespect to you, Alex, but it is small fry for us so it's not an area we've focused on. Be my guest, for the usual fee."

"That goes without saying, Frank. Of course, I will show you the appropriate consideration. Despite what McCarthy might have thought, we are not all communists just because we live on the West Coast."

Frank smiled.

"And that is the joke people up in the Hollywood Hills still don't find funny. I wish you well with your new endeavor. Let me know if you need my assistance at any point."

THE PARTY WAS in full swing and Alex found himself standing with a Scotch in his hand talking to Frank Sinatra. The guy had the ear of Sam Giancana, so Alex knew he could be trusted, and he understood why Alex was attending this Hollywood shindig: to catch some customers in his web.

Not that he had a problem with Sinatra. Unbeknownst to the crooner and actor, their paths had first crossed at the Havana conference back in the '40s when the heads of the syndicate had met to decide the fate of Benny Siegel.

The singer had performed on the first night. Then every time Sinatra had performed in one of the Cuban hotels owned by Lansky, Giancana, or Trafficante, Alex had been in the audience or in the group that had gone out for dinner the same evening. Now they were chatting like old friends, while the whole of Hollywood cavorted around them.

"How long are you going to be in town, Alex?"

"I moved into Boyle Heights this month, so you'll be seeing a lot more of me."

"Always a pleasure, never a chore. You know that. Is there anything I can get for you?"

Alex recalled this gathering was in Frank's place. He raised his tumbler and said, "I'm good, thanks."

"That's not what I meant, Alex. Can I get you *anything*?"

Frank's hand swept around the room, palm up, and if Alex didn't mistake the gesture, it appeared as though the fella's fingers lingered only on the women in the room. Alex's cheeks tingled for a moment and he ground his molars.

"Not for me, thanks. Quite the reverse. If you know of anyone who needs a companion for the evening, then let me know in future."

Sinatra returned his hand to his side and stared at Alex for a long second. Then he nodded.

"Sure thing, Alex. I hold a party only once a season, but I will bear that in mind."

"And tell your friends the offer's good for them too."

Another nod.

"Let me introduce you to some of my buddies, Alex. You know the rat pack, but there are plenty more names you can put to faces."

Alex smiled and followed Frank around the room, but he didn't have the heart to tell him he didn't bother with the movies unless it was a good Western.

◆ ◆ ◆

AN HOUR LATER and Alex had only worked half the party. He recognized most of the names he heard and made a special detour to pass by Ginger Rogers and say hello, but he feigned sufficient concern over the lives of the others to make tens of new friends.

One face that he knew was attached to a curvaceous body and a shock of platinum blond hair. Alex reckoned he had nothing to lose and sauntered over to her and the guy she was with. "Sorry to interrupt, but I just wanted to say how much I love your work." Then he turned to walk elsewhere.

"Hey, bud. Thank you for saying so but there's no need to run away."

Alex stopped, sipped his Scotch, and introduced himself.

"Thanks, Marilyn."

"Tell me, which of my performances did you appreciate the most?"

Alex's mind went blank. Just because he recognized Marilyn Monroe did not mean he'd seen any of her films.

"Some Like It Hot?"

She scowled, and he realized he had said the wrong thing, but he'd heard Sarah talk about it because it was about the St Valentine's Day massacre, and Alex had had a hand in that. That's why it stuck in his head. It was time to deflect the conversation in a different direction.

"And I don't think I've met your friend."

Marilyn's expression relaxed when she turned to the man by her side.

"This is Jack."

"Pleased to meet you, Senator."

The guy had a firm handshake and as soon as he let go, Jack picked the cigarette from Marilyn's hand, exhaled, and took three short tokes. Then he passed it back to Marilyn, who inhaled as deeply herself before offering the roach to Alex, who declined the opportunity to smoke the Mary Jane.

"Call me Jack. No need to be formal when we are among friends."

"I knew your predecessor: Merrick Townsend. He represents New Jersey nowadays."

"Great guy."

With that, Kennedy took Marilyn by the hand and wandered off to the other side of the room to get some more drinks, but Alex saw what had just happened and tried to decide whether the politician had figured out who he was before he blanked him.

A GLANCE AT his tumbler told Alex he needed a refill, so he waited for Jack and Marilyn to move away from the bar then zigzagged over to get a fresh Scotch. As he collected his liquor, a woman sidled up to him and ordered a glass of white wine. He felt her leaning in so their hips touched. Alex turned to face her and clinked glasses.

"Haven't we met somewhere before?"

"If that's your best line, Mac, you're going to have to try much harder."

Alex responded to her comment with a blank expression.

"My name is Alex Cohen, and I meant we met in Havana; at the opening of a casino or hotel. I can't remember which one."

"Sorry, Alex. I misunderstood. Your face is familiar. Call me Lana."

Memories of refusing credit to Turner's then-boyfriend, Johnny Stompanato, flooded into Alex's memory.

"Sorry about all the trouble you've had, Lana."

She stiffened her back and then let her shoulders sag as she exhaled.

"Sometimes you gotta deal with a situation. Do you have anything to smoke?"

Alex fumbled in his pockets until he produced a packet of cigarettes and flicked at the end of the pack to make one pop out of the aperture at the top.

"Not quite what I meant, but thank you, Alex, anyway."

"I don't keep anything stronger on me, but if you tell me what you'd like, then I can always get you a regular supply."

"Whoa, fella. We might have attended the same opening night for Meyer Lansky, but that doesn't make us pals."

"Never said that it did, Lana. It's just that I am new in town and I'm looking to expand my activities in Burbank. Ask Frank about me and maybe we can talk some other time."

"You're a friend of Sinatra?"

Alex nodded and smiled.

"In that case, we can probably do business."

3

ALEX VISITED HIS sons Moishe and David, along with sister Esther, in New York as much to see the family as to talk about his legitimate business interests.

"We haven't seen you since you got back to the US. How was it getting out of Cuba?"

"A few hairy moments, but all was fine, Esther. You're looking good."

"I like the taste of Bowery air in my lungs."

Moishe chortled, and Esther threw him a glance.

"Something amuses you, my boy?"

"No, Pop. How was the journey over?"

"Nothing much to report. The good thing is that it didn't take as long as it used to."

"We live in modern times, Pop."

"Is it too early for me to invite you guys out to lunch?"

Esther had a quick look at the clock on the wall and shook her head.

"If it's somewhere swanky, then we're ready to go now."

"Grab your coats. Let's hop over to the Waldorf-Astoria."

Alex's limo took the group uptown in no time at all, and soon they were ensconced in the five-star luxury to which Alex was very much accustomed. Esther's eyes popped out of their sockets when she looked around the restaurant.

"I don't think I've ever seen so much mink on so many shoulders."

"It makes you wonder how their men got the cash to afford them."

"You are a cynic, David Cohen."

His lawyer son glanced at Alex to show his understanding of how gelt operated in this town. Moishe added his own perspective. "This just goes to show what hard work can achieve."

He looked round at his lunch companions and they all laughed.

"Gelt makes gelt and nothing more," intoned Alex as they settled into their menus.

Once the waiter took their order, Alex turned to what was uppermost on his mind.

"How have you all been?"

"Alex, married life is treating your two sons well and I am much happier since you last saw me."

He smiled at his sister and recalled picking her up with David and dragging her back to her room in Havana. The woman had almost drowned in a bottle of tequila.

"That's good. And Mama?"

"She is slowing down, of course, but she is well, Pop."

Alex wondered what stopped him from visiting her himself. There was time this trip, but he knew he would not do so.

ON HIS WAY over to Hoboken, Alex pondered why it had taken him so long to visit his New York operations. Moishe was right, Havana had been a year ago and all he had achieved since then was to sit on his *tuches* and grow fat. He looked down at his paunch and realized that he might be exaggerating. He wondered to what extent his mind had slowed down in the past twelve months. He was getting old, minute by minute, day by day.

The limo pulled up to a nondescript building in central Hoboken, only six blocks from Alex's former apartment, where the boys would come to stay when they were kids. He got out and entered the lobby to be met by a receptionist, who eyed him up and down for a moment.

"I'm here to speak with Merrick Townsend."

"Is he expecting you, sir?"

"Not at all, but if you let him know I am here, then he will see me."

The pinhead looked at Alex through the bottom of his eyeglasses and pretended to hide his disdain.

"Mr. Townsend does not meet with uninvited guests."

"You should put a call through to his assistant and let her know that Alex Cohen is here to see Merrick."

He held the gaze of the receptionist for a couple of seconds until the guy got uncomfortable. Alex looked around the counter and spotted a name etched into a bronze-colored plate.

"Mr. Garfield. Aiden. I understand many people walk off the street and demand to speak with Merrick. I imagine part of your role is to distinguish these individuals from those who should meet with him. You need to verify that I belong to the second category. You will achieve this by speaking with Merrick's secretary."

Garfield's eyes flitted left then right, and a hand edged toward the phone on the desk.

"Bear with me while I speak with Mr. Townsend's assistant."

Alex smirked and stepped back to allow Garfield to retain what remained of his dignity. Two minutes later, he sat down in Townsend's anteroom with a coffee and an apology from Amy Penn about the wait before Mr. Townsend was ready to see him.

"THANK YOU FOR seeing me, Merrick."

"It is always a pleasure, Alex."

"As I was passing by, I thought I'd drop in. How's tricks?"

"Can't complain. My constituents keep me pretty busy. You know how it is."

"And how are Sylvia and your kids?"

"She is fine, and they have grown up fast."

"Tell me about it, Merrick. My two eldest work for me nowadays."

"You have others?"

"Three, but we haven't spoken for years…"

Merrick allowed Alex to dwell on that thought for a short beat, but that was long enough.

"How long are you planning on being in town? As lovely as it is to see you, I have a schedule, but I can meet up with you for dinner any night this week."

Alex nodded and opened his briefcase, fumbled around inside, and pulled out a dossier. Then he placed it on Townsend's desk, although the senator did nothing with it, apart from giving it a second glance.

"Like I said, Merrick, I'm only passing through, so now is the time when we need to talk."

Townsend leaned back in his swivel chair and lit a cigar after offering Alex one. When he looked at the item in his hand, he noticed they were Cuban and smiled at the irony.

"Let's get this over with then."

"Merrick, I'd like you to do me a favor."

"You know I am always happy to help. What do you need?"

"I want you to introduce me to Jack Kennedy."

Townsend stiffened and attempted to hide his reaction by tapping some ash into the ashtray.

"The guy is trying to become the Democratic nominee for the presidency. With the greatest respect, Alex, I don't think he is going to want to have a conversation with a man of your… pedigree."

"Open the file, Merrick."

Alex waited for Townsend to follow his instructions and then to digest the contents of the Manila envelope.

"May I remind you that the photo was taken on the night when you were in Havana and found Lupita Alfaro sliced to ribbons by the scissors from your hotel room."

Townsend swallowed hard.

"Then you phoned for my help to deal with the murdered prostitute. We resolved all those issues, and I told you that, in the future, I would ask you for a favor. You appear to have forgotten our arrangement, but the picture in your hand has jogged your memory, judging by your expression. You can keep the photo if you like. I have many more copies in case of need."

"She was the sweetest girl I have ever met. There isn't a day that goes by without me thinking about her."

"Touching, but I saw her body that night and there wasn't much care being shown by you with that *nafka*."

Townsend's eyes bore into Alex like he'd just sliced his mother's face open, but the only violence had been perpetrated by Senator Merrick Townsend. And they both knew it.

4

RATHER THAN TRAVEL all the way to the West Coast before heading back to the commonwealth of Massachusetts, Alex took the sensible decision of going straight to Boston to wait a day or so before he could visit Kennedy.

Sure enough, a call from the senator's people relayed the message that the presidential nominee had made time in his schedule for Alex to see him that afternoon for fifteen minutes.

Kennedy's election office was a storefront building nestled among a crowd of mom-and-pop mercantile opportunities for the hapless shopper, near Charles Street and Jefferson. As Alex headed for the entrance, the hustle of campaign workers was all around him.

Out of the corner of his eye, he spotted Marilyn Monroe's boyfriend as he scurried from one side of the building to the other and ducked into an office with a glass wall and blinds for privacy. Alex followed him in.

"Good to see you again, Jack."

Kennedy looked up from the pile of papers he had brought in with him and squinted at Alex.

"We met at Frank Sinatra's party a few weeks back. Don't tell me you've forgotten the thirty-second conversation we had together. It's etched on my memory forever."

Alex proffered his hand and Kennedy shook it like a well-conditioned politician should.

"I'm sorry. You are…?"

"Alex Cohen, Jack. Your people gave me fifteen minutes with you now. You appear confused."

Kennedy stood up, walked out, and shouted for someone to find his schedule. A woman appeared clutching a diary and confirmed the appointment. Kennedy shrugged and returned to sit behind his desk.

"Alex, you have my attention. What can I do for you?"

"First, do you remember Frank's party?"

Kennedy stared into the middle distance and shrugged again.

"I go to a lot of parties. I can't say that any spring to mind right now, but I believe you when you state we met there."

"That's fine, Jack. I only ask because you were sharing a marijuana cigarette with Marilyn Monroe."

Kennedy stiffened, exhaled, and closed the blinds on the glass wall.

"Is this some kind of shakedown or has one of the boys sent you to pull my leg?"

"Neither, Jack. Judging from your reaction though, your memory of the party is improving."

"Don't get fresh with me, Mac."

"The name is Alex and I have a business proposition for you."

"Sounds like extortion to me."

"Such harsh words, Jack, and I have done nothing to you to deserve your mistrust. Far from it. At any point since we met, I could have gone to the papers or the Republicans and inform them of what I saw you do, but I have refrained from such action. Do you know why, Jack?"

"Why, Alex?"

"Because I want to help you win the election. Who knows how far this country will go with you at the helm?"

"You mentioned a business proposition."

"We don't get nothing for nothing in this life, as I am sure you are aware, Jack. I propose boosting your election war chest in exchange for your help with my winning state construction contracts."

Jack Kennedy's glare softened at hearing Alex's offer. Politicians are the same the world over: they want power and aren't that fussy about how they gain it.

"And I suppose the amount of your financial contribution will be less than the value of the building contracts?"

"Let's just say that the more you let me dip my beak in the trough, then the greater my generosity. And, of course, my friends will be eager to support you too."

"Money is always welcome."

"Jack, when I was a kid, my mentor Waxey Gordon had a close relationship with the New York Democratic Party. He didn't put cash in their pockets, but there were other ways he found to help. My business partners will find other forms of support for your campaign efforts."

The senator leaned his elbows on the desk and rested his chin on his palms.

"Are you offering to stuff ballots for me?"

"Jack, I am letting you know that if you help me get state construction contracts, then I will ensure that my friends assist in the election, assuming you get the party nomination."

Kennedy grinned.

"So your money gets me the nomination and your friends deliver me the White House?"

"That's the size of it."

"What makes you think I need that much help?"

"Perhaps you don't. To be honest, I don't follow politics. I have never found the law to be a friend of mine and the people who make laws are of even less concern to me."

Kennedy shuffled in his seat as though the act of being in the room with Alex caused him discomfort.

"But I look across your campaign headquarters and I see a bunch of college kids running around like their asses are on fire. This is not how a winning team behaves, so I would guess that you might welcome my suggestion. Also, the fact you continue with this conversation shows you have some minimal interest in what I have to say."

Kennedy shuffled some more and then stood up and said, "Excuse me one minute," before scurrying out of his office, leaving Alex on his own and unsure what to make of this erratic behavior.

True to his word, Kennedy came back and settled back into his seat.

"Apologies, but I am taking new meds and they are disagreeing with me. You were saying?"

"Let me cut to the chase, Jack. You need me far more than I need you. To make matters clear, I have known many Catholics in my life and, while I am not of that faith myself, I imagine your voters would be unimpressed with a candidate who smoked illegal substances and had an extramarital affair."

Alex lit a cigarette to give Kennedy time to mull over what he'd heard. After three long drags, Alex noticed there was no ashtray. Instead, he leaned forward and grabbed a coffee mug on the desk, peeked inside to find the dregs of Kennedy's last cup, and flicked the ash in it. The man sat opposite him scowled but did nothing to object.

Throughout the time that Alex took to finish his smoke, Jack Kennedy averted his gaze. Alex thought he heard cogs whirring in the man's skull.

"Well?"

"Alex, I have met your kind before and I have never enjoyed the experience."

"I am not asking for us to be friends, but to be business associates."

"Let me finish. Like my father before me, I understand how politics operates; sometimes you have unusual bedfellows. My brother, Robert, sees the world in black and white, whereas I live in the penumbra."

"Gray is my favorite color."

"Alex, if you can deliver what you say, then we have a deal. If you fail me, then you must understand I will call the FBI and they'll cart you to jail."

"Prison isn't that bad, Jack. It's the waiting to get out that'll hang you every time."

"And I suppose you'd know about that, wouldn't you?"

"Jack, don't be so hasty to judge a man. What I do is put bread on my family's table and provide a roof under which they can sleep safe at night. The only difference between you and me is that you care what people think of you. I only care about results."

Kennedy maintained the smile he'd plastered across his face since he returned from the john.

"By the way, Jack. The next time you are visiting Marilyn, let me know and I can supply you with anything to make the party go with a swing, from a discreet venue to grass and coke."

"If I ever pass that way again, I'll bear that offer in mind."

The grin somehow got broader and Jack's chest puffed out.

"And, you never know, I might have a different girl in tow."

"What you do in the privacy of someone else's home is of no concern to me. Like I told you, I don't follow politics and I do not care about the private lives of politicians. It's what you do that matters most to me, Jack. I shall judge you on your actions."

"In that case, we will get along just fine. Give me your contact details and next week you'll receive a call. That'll be for the first contract. If you send a check to my campaign the same day, then we both know the deal is sound. If not, you can kiss my ass."

APRIL 1961

5

SARAH AND ALEX settled into a simple routine. In the mornings, they enjoyed breakfast together, on the patio if the weather was in their favor. Then Alex would hustle into his recently built office and she remained in the main house. Together for lunch and then they'd take Alex's limo over to Burbank to attend to business in the afternoon and evening.

"To what extent do you trust your coke connection, Alex?"

"He appears to have been reliable since DeSimone introduced us last year. Why do you ask?"

"There's a discrepancy in the books between the amount you've paid for and the quantity you have received. It might not be much, but if you look after the pennies…"

Alex tilted his head and smiled.

"I will check that out, hon'."

"There might be nothing to find apart from poor record keeping on our part."

"Sarah, you mean me, don't you?"

"Alex, I'm not accusing anybody yet."

"Only a matter of time, though, right?"

"Listen, mister. I wouldn't put it past you not to note every few bags you receive, but if it becomes a habit, then we'll never see if we make any money at this game."

Now it was Alex's turn to smile.

"And I was running drugs while you were changing diapers."

"That is very true, but you still need to record what you buy and sell if you want me to look after the books."

"Remind me again, why we are keeping such excellent notes of our criminal activities. If the FBI gets hold of this paperwork, then I'm sunk."

"Alex, we must ensure we make money. And there is only one copy of these records. The only way the Feds can get their hands on them will be over my dead body and if that is the case, then you've got more to worry about than a tax fraud investigation."

He drew on his cigarette and nodded, not wanting to think too much about the implication of Sarah's words.

"Let me change the subject as I don't like the way the last one was heading. How are the girls?"

Sarah leaned back in her chair and sighed.

"Everything is going all right. The two cathouses we own are doing solid business. From what I've calculated, every bedroom has a nafka on her back for at least twelve hours a day."

"And how's the Hollywood party scene?"

"Less productive. It's a function of the number of parties and how many hosts we know and deal with. The problem we have is that everybody wants to do a line of white powder but only a small proportion want to have call girls hanging around A-list stars. They think it'll cramp their style."

"It's the lonely headline acts that are grateful for the attention without needing to worry about anybody growing any attachments."

"You don't have to convince me, Alex. It's the likes of Sinatra who needs to hear your sales pitch."

Alex laughed because they both knew that Frank would do anything to keep on the right side of the mob and had been requesting a steady supply of ass every time he held one of his parties. It was the rest of the rat pack that needed to be turned. If they all sourced tail from Alex, then other actors in Hollywood would follow suit.

◆ ◆ ◆

HOW LUCKY WAS Alex to bump into Peter Langford the next day as he arrived at the movie studio to film some interiors for a new Sinatra picture? He made sure he parked right by Langford so they could walk and talk until they reached the sound stage.

"What brings you round these parts, Alex?"

"Haven't you heard? I'm back on the West Coast. Sarah and I came over more than a year ago. I thought you might have spotted me at the far end of the room at one of Frank's parties."

"I'm afraid not, but you're not the sort I'm sniffing out when there's a party in full swing, if you get my meaning."

"Sure do, and no offense taken. You're looking out for someone younger and prettier all round."

Peter guffawed.

"You know me too well, Alex. Now if you could guarantee you had a juicy skirt with you, then I'd give you the time of day at least."

Both men chortled and Alex stroked his chin.

"Now that you mention it, I might be able to help you in that regard. When're you going to your next party?"

"Saturday, of course. Why?"

"How would you like me to introduce you to a lovely girl you can drape over your arm when you walk in the door?"

"With my reputation, Alex, it's not getting the girl that's a problem. They are like moths at night and have the habit of skipping around, flapping away at every light they see in the room."

"This is where the individual I find for you will be more than perfect. Not only can you be certain that she'll make you salivate when you see her, but you can bet your bottom dollar she'll leave with you too."

Peter stopped in his tracks and tilted his head as he thought through Alex's promise. Then he smiled and slapped Alex on the back.

"If you could do that for me, I will make you a rich man."

"I hope you will. And if you need anything to keep the buzz going, tell me because I can obtain substances you can't get in your local pharmacy."

A wink told Langford all he needed to know, and they shook hands.

"If you have a good time on Saturday, then inform your friends because there's plenty of ass to go round and more coke than you can inhale."

Peter bid Alex farewell and entered the stage to tell the rest of the rat pack what Alex was offering. He popped into the studio canteen for a quick coffee and then drove back to the office to let Sarah know they had a special booking.

DAVID HAD BEEN staying in a guest bedroom for the past three months since he'd arrived from New York.

"Tell me, Pop. You don't appear to have much work for me to do."

David, Alex, and Sarah sat in the living room after dinner, a glass of their favorite liquor in their hand.

"Son, the problem is that I am not investing in anything that you can put your hands on."

"Did you tell me that so I wouldn't ask how the family operation is doing?"

"No, I said it so that you would understand why there isn't much for you right now. The only thing I can think of is the operation that flows through New York."

"When I came here, I thought you were preparing to keep only your legal activities. When we fled Havana, you said you wanted to retire and leave the criminal life behind you."

"Almost, David. I announced I wished to go legit but informed you all that I was going to Florida to seek opportunities with Santo Trafficante, who is a man not untainted by the mob. He represents the mafia in that state."

David swilled the brandy in his glass.

"Are you pushing me out, Pop?"

Alex swallowed hard.

"That is not my intention, but we both know I must protect you from some of my business affairs. You cannot be a party to matters which would get you disbarred."

His son took a swig of his cognac.

"I understand, but I am not the least happy about it."

"Of course you are not, but don't forget the importance I place on having you look after Esther and Moishe. They are both meticulous with detail but too naïve in the dark art of business. You must mentor your brother more and make sure your aunt remains sober."

"She hasn't touched a drop since she left Cuba. Those days are passed."

Alex nodded and glanced at Sarah, who remained silent throughout the entire exchange.

IN BED THAT night, just after he switched the light off, Alex turned to Sarah.

"I'd be much happier if David stayed in California, wouldn't you?"

"Of course. The mother hen in me would love it if all my chicks lived near the nest."

"That's not quite what I meant."

"I know, Alex, but you want to have your cake and eat it. Either involve David in all your dealings or clean up your act."

"I can't do that yet. You know that."

"Alex, that is what you believe, and so that is how you behave. Don't tell me you couldn't get a fair price for your Las Vegas interests and for the import/export from Italy."

"Perhaps…"

"And we only have cathouses and drug supply in Hollywood to give ourselves something to do if we are being honest with ourselves. Right?"

"Maybe…"

"So, the only thing stopping you from keeping David in Los Angeles are the decisions you make."

"For sure, hon'."

"The choice is yours. Send David back to New York or sell your more salacious enterprises."

6

TWO WEEKS AFTER David flew back to LaGuardia, Alex heard Jack was in town, so he paid a visit to Jayne Mansfield.

"Do you have any plans for the weekend, Jayne?"

"There is no need to be coy, Alex. We both know I am spending time with Jack."

"And you know that I'm the go-to guy for anyone planning a party that's going to last the entire weekend."

"Alex, why do you think I took your call?"

"I'm flattered, Jayne. What do you need and when would you like me to deliver it?"

"My usual order will be more than ample."

"That's fine. When shall I come over?"

ALEX ARRIVED AT eight, just as he'd promised Jayne he would. He rang the doorbell and waited for thirty seconds until she answered the door with a smile and swanned back to her living room, leaving Alex to close the door behind himself. He followed her inside and stopped in his tracks when he saw Jack on the couch in the pinkest place he had ever seen.

"Good evening, Mr. President."

"Call me Jack when I'm not representing the office of the presidency."

"Congratulations, by the way. This is the first time we've spoken since you won the White House."

"Thank you, and for all your support."

"We made an agreement and I always keep my word, Jack."

"How's the construction business round here? Still doing well?"

"You know that I was only the front for those contracts. They've been putting up buildings ever since the Romans."

"I thought that was the Greeks, Alex?"

"I don't know any Greeks, only Italians."

They both smiled while Jayne removed the contents of the bag Alex had dropped on a nearby sideboard. She tapped some powder onto a mirror on a coffee table by Jack's perch on the couch. Then she cut it up repeatedly until she had four lines arranged. With an arm resting on Jack's lap, Jayne took a curled-up Jackson and snorted one line. Then she swapped nostrils and inhaled the second.

Mansfield passed the note over to Jack, who pushed her off his leg in order to bend forward and take the two remaining tramlines for himself. He looked up at Alex and shrugged. "Nothing for you, Alex," and sniggered.

"I don't imbibe. Thanks anyway, but I would like a quiet word as we've bumped into each other."

"Now is not the time, Alex. I can't tell you how wide of the mark you are at the minute."

"Shall I come back tomorrow afternoon?"

"Whatever…"

As Alex turned to leave Jayne's house, she hauled herself off the floor and slithered onto Jack's lap. They started making out, and Alex closed the door.

AS PROMISED, HE swung by the Sunset Boulevard mansion Saturday around three to start up the failed conversation from the night before. When he rang the bell, this time Jayne took at least a minute to get to the door. She was wrapped in only a bathrobe, which left very little to the imagination. She beckoned Alex in and he padded upstairs to discover that the living room was not alone in being painted pink. He didn't think there was an inch of wall that had any other color on it.

Jayne vanished into a bedroom and Alex followed her, wary of what state of undress he might find the president of the free world in. A flush of the john and Jack emerged from the en suite wearing a matching bathrobe.

She lit a cigarette and passed it over to him, before sitting on the bed. Jack nestled next to her and rested a hand over her thighs. Alex tried to decide whether the man would have done the same if he hadn't been in the room and realized he didn't care. If Kennedy was playing games to make him feel uncomfortable, then it wouldn't work. Alex had seen much more and far worse over the years.

"Take a seat, Alex, if you are going to stay."

"Last night we agreed we would use this afternoon to talk business."

"That's not what was said, but I'll let it go for now."

"Jayne, do you mind rustling us up some coffee?"

The actress smiled at Alex's suggestion but looked at Jack, who nodded consent to give her permission to leave.

"I understand you want to build on our past business relationship, Alex, but your timing is lousy. I only have a few more hours before I am expected back to my work and no matter how enjoyable a conversation with you might be, it pales into insignificance compared to the pleasure I can derive from the same time spent between Jayne's thighs."

"Does your wife know about Jayne?"

"Don't be impertinent."

"I meant no disrespect, Jack. My only thought was whether you had an open marriage, and nothing more. I don't read the comics, so I do not know what gossip is out there about you. I appreciate what it's like to find out about yourself in the dailies and it is never pleasant."

Kennedy's shoulders sagged, and he inhaled on his cigarette.

"No offense taken. I thought you were trying to do a cheap hustle on me… but, I keep my infidelities private."

"The papers are silent so I figured as much."

"Alex, it's time for you to go. Talk to me on some other occasion, but not when I am only wearing a bathrobe in Jayne Mansfield's bedroom."

SINATRA INVITED ALEX to spend a few days at the Cal Neva Lodge as there was someone Sinatra thought he would like to meet. Although the proposal sounded mysterious, Frank wouldn't have wasted his time, so he kissed Sarah goodbye and headed for the lodge, which was on the border of California and Nevada, as its name implied.

The first night he checked in, Alex hit the restaurant. Frank popped over to welcome him to the establishment and they chatted for a short while before the singer flitted off to another table for more schmoozing.

Alex had spent his entire life sitting at the rear of restaurants, in the shadows, but tonight the maître d' had positioned him in the middle of the place. Alex monitored Sinatra as he worked the room. With whom did he spend the most time? A booth at the back housing a man and a woman. The guy was too far into the darkness for Alex to see and although he had never met the young woman before, she had all the marks of a good-time girl and nothing more.

He might have only given Alex five minutes, but the guy received a half hour's attention. As Frank got up to leave, the man leaned forward and his head emerged from the shadowy darkness. Alex understood why he had got more attention; Jack Kennedy was a far more important person than Alex could ever be.

Once the couple had finished eating and the busboy had cleared their table, Alex watched Jack call for the check. As they walked past Alex, Jack stopped to talk, an arm hanging around the skirt's neck.

"Good to see you, Alex. How's tricks?"

"All fine, thank you for asking, but we never completed our conversation from the last time we met."

Kennedy stared back with not even a flicker of recognition in his expression.

"My friend and I are about to have a nightcap. Care to join us?"

Alex looked down at his plate and calculated how long it would take him to eat a third of a steak.

"I'll be ten minutes. Will you be at the bar on this floor?"

A nod from Jack and he sauntered off. His arm slipped off the girl's shoulder and landed on her butt cheek. When you are president, you don't have to worry too much about what a woman thinks of your clumsy moves.

ALEX CAUGHT UP with the happy couple fifteen minutes later when he aimed for a back booth in the hotel's second-floor bar. The lovebirds were cooing when he arrived and he sat opposite them, facing Kennedy.

"Aren't you going to introduce me to your friend?"

"No, babe. There's no need for that. Why don't you powder your nose?"

The girl smiled and left. All the while, Alex watched Jack stare at her ass as it wiggled away.

"I'm looking forward to finishing this drink, you know what I mean?"

"Sure do, Jack. You are one lucky man."

"Luck has nothing to do with it. I earned that the hard way."

Alex couldn't be bothered to argue with the guy and was more concerned with business.

"Now you've left Massachusetts, new construction contracts have trailed off. So I am hoping you will agree to a more relevant arrangement as you have some sway with federal opportunities."

Jack maintained the grin that had appeared on his face from the moment he'd stared at the disappearing ass.

"Alex, we had an agreement, and we both held up our end of the bargain, but that moment is over and there's nothing more to be said."

It was Alex's turn to smile.

"Jack, I understand why you might think that is the case. However, we have become business partners and that relationship persists until the end of time. So I have a new proposal for you."

"I'm listening."

"You swing some federal contracts my way so that my Italian friends can benefit too, and I will ensure that your liaisons remain private from the general public and from your wife. I've met many politicians in my time, but the devout Catholic ones don't go to hotels and have clandestine meetings with cocktail waitresses."

"She's not a waitress. Cheryl is an actress."

"Jack, what she does for a living is of no concern to me. She could be a whore for all I care. The fact remains that you shouldn't be sleeping with her. Do we have a deal?"

Cheryl waddled back to their table in her red stilettos and matching pencil skirt. Jack's eyes continued to pop outside his head. Then he turned to Alex.

"Yes. Now leave me alone to enjoy the delights of this fabulous woman."

They shook hands and as he stood up, Alex bent to whisper in Jack's ear. "Remember to tip her well. Loose talk costs careers."

7

ALEX HAD ONLY been back home three weeks before Santo Trafficante called him and invited him to come to Florida as his guest. That afternoon, a private plane took him from LA to Fort Lauderdale, where a limo ferried him over to Boca Raton. The sun was setting by the time he arrived at a warehouse on the edge of town.

As he entered the building, the saloon turned round and drove off. Alex swallowed hard and licked his lips. All was quiet within those walls and no lights were on, despite the fading sunlight. He kept the creaking door open to minimize the noisy announcement of his arrival, but Alex knew Santo would hear he was there.

He tiptoed through the reception area and wondered where the welcoming committee had got to. Then Alex halted in his tracks and the thought crossed his mind that Santo had drawn him here for darker reasons. Alex had lost count of the number of times he had brought people into similar warehouses to drag them out in a makeshift body bag. Was he about to meet the same fate?

He pushed at a door in the far wall and walked into a large space with some kind of machinery fifty feet away, but it was too dark to make out any details. To the left and right were row upon row of shelving and in front of him was an empty area, comprising only a table and a few chairs. A man in silhouette sat there with a cigarette in his hands.

"Thank you for agreeing to see me, Alex."

Santo's voice was quiet and almost monotone, and a hand showed for him to step forward and join the old Italian gangster at the table. He walked toward Trafficante, where a pot of coffee and three mugs were waiting for him.

"Are we expecting anyone else?"

"No. Why do you ask?"

Alex pointed at the third mug and Santo explained everything by flicking his ash into the receptacle.

"There's no need to make a mess in your own place, is there, Alex?"

"I don't suppose there is, Santo. Could we not have met somewhere less... stark?"

The fella inhaled his cigarette before dropping it into the trash-mug.

"Until we have had this conversation and I find out if you are interested in my proposal, then this meeting never happened and the fewer people who see you in the state, the better."

"Now you have me intrigued, Santo: spill."

"If you ignore the end, we had fabulous times in Cuba, wouldn't you say?"

"Sure. We were hotel neighbors and did good business together."

"That's what I thought too. You and I have had no beef either have we?"

"No, I can't say that we have, Santo. But why this interest in reliving the past? What's done is done."

"It is, and it isn't. A friend of mine has asked for my assistance and I think you can help me with his request."

Alex exhaled.

"Is there a hit you want me to do? Because if there is, let's talk about it without hiding in a crummy warehouse in the middle of nowhere."

Santo raised a smile and shook his head.

"Close, but no cigar. My acquaintance would like some help in Cuba. Would you be prepared to go back there for a short while? A few days only."

"Thank you for thinking of me, but Santo, I am too old to be gallivanting around that island to rob a bank or whatever you have planned. I prefer easier ways to make my money nowadays."

"Oh no, Alex. We don't want to hit a savings and loan. Nothing as tawdry as that. We wish to take out Castro."

"Whack him?"

"Yep."

"Santo, you and whose army?"

Trafficante lit another cigarette and offered one to Alex.

"We were thinking you would recruit your own army. Well, troop of men anyway."

"And do what? Fly over to Cuba, parachute in, and assassinate Fidel Castro?"

"Plane, boat. How you do it is less important right now than whether you're prepared to try."

Alex smoked his entire cigarette in silence until he inhaled roach and he tossed it into the mug. Santo poured them another cup of dark brown coffee each.

"Who's behind this? What is the name of your friend?"

"If you are in, then I will tell you, but we can't afford for anyone to know if they are not involved. It's for your own good."

"No can do, Santo. With all due respect, if you want me to kill a foreign leader, I must have the name of the person who is paying my wages."

Santo thought for a moment, then nodded.

"It is a mutual friend. A man of power."

Alex stared at the Italian, none the wiser. Santo snorted his disappointment.

"Jack Kennedy, you dolt."

"I thought the CIA did covert operations."

"They do, but Kennedy has asked us to help because we've lived in Cuba and we are renowned for successful hits."

"And you want me to work with the CIA to assassinate Castro?"

"They've recruited an army of exiles in Miami and are training them in Guatemala."

"So what do they need me for?"

"You have military experience and you know the island, the towns, the streets. Besides which, this wouldn't be your first assassination and we need somebody cool in the face of enemy fire when we kill that bastard."

"And why haven't the CIA come to me directly? What skin do you have in this game?"

"Alex, let's just say that Jack and I have reached an understanding, a working relationship you might call it."

"I have a similar set-up with him too."

"We would all like to return to the casino business in Havana. And Kennedy wants a base in the Caribbean that relies on the US for its success. Jack wins, the mob wins, and so do you. What's not to like?"

"How much to kill Castro?"

"Half a million to cover your expenses. And another half on his death."

"What if we fail?"

"Then you don't get the second payment."

"And I'll come home in a body bag."

"If you are lucky, Alex. Yes."

"I hope you don't expect an answer tonight, because I need to think this through before I respond."

"Take all the time you need. I'll get some food and bedding delivered here."

"No, Santo. I need to leave this place. There is no way I can think properly cooped up in this excuse for accommodation. I shall hole up somewhere discreet, but I am not staying here. Trust me on this."

"You have two days. If word gets out about this operation, then I will know it was you who spilled your guts."

"Santo, there's no need for such words. I understand the responsibility of omertà. If I didn't squawk to the cops when I was in Sing Sing, why would I start now?"

"Just remember that Kennedy is a man we can work with. He is pliable and open to sensible business arrangements."

"That I know for myself, Santo."

"And by keeping Jack close, we get him to place brother Bobby on a short leash. That guy wants to take down organized crime."

Santo laughed aloud but before Alex joined in, Trafficante stopped and looked dead-eyed into his Cuban neighbor.

"And we can't let that happen, can we, Alex?"

8

"GOOD TO SEE you, Alex. Come on in."

He smiled at Thelma Lansky and followed her as she took him up to the guest bedroom. When he came downstairs, she showed him to the living room where Meyer was watching the baseball on television.

"The Minnesota Twins are making short change of the Yankees."

Alex nodded and sat in an easy chair while his friend enjoyed the game, although, for a lifelong Yankees fan, the result was about as bad as it could be.

"To think they've only just come up from Washington. You'd imagine the Twins would be tired from the journey."

The problem was that Alex knew little of the rules of baseball and was even less interested in discussing it, given what Santo had asked him to do.

"I need to stay a night or two, Meyer, if that's all right with you and Thelma."

"That woman is a peach."

"Meyer, I have an important decision to make and I came here because I value your opinion. Do you mind if we switch the TV off?"

Meyer suggested they take a walk around the block, but Alex explained he had promised not to be seen on the streets.

"This is sounding dangerous before you've even told me what is going on, Alex."

"Right now, I'm in the clear, but there is a lot riding on this if I agree to Santo's proposal."

"Is he involved? The *meeskait*."

"You and he have done enough business together over the years. Is he such a bad fella to work with?"

"You know my feeling about the Italians so don't get me started."

Meyer led Alex out through the patio doors and to a table and chairs by the pool.

"You swim, Meyer?"

"Of course not. It's for Thelma, and the kids if they ever visit. But you know what it's like—they don't write, they don't phone…"

A nod and Alex allowed the conversation to slide into oblivion so he could keep Meyer onside. They soaked in the warmth of the sun and enjoyed each other's company, talking about nothing as Lansky seemed unable to focus on anything serious.

AFTER DINNER, THELMA left the men alone after she had washed up the dishes and headed into the living room. Meyer and Alex wandered back to the patio.

"I'm visiting you because I am interested in your opinion, and you know all the parties involved."

"Is this the Santo business?"

"Yes, Meyer. He approached me and asked me to help him take Cuba from the revolutionaries."

Meyer almost spat his coffee back into his mug.

"Are you serious? What does that Italian think you're going to do? Fly over, parachute in, and assassinate Castro?"

Alex laughed.

"That is one plan on the table, from what I hear, but the bigger issue is whether I should do it at all."

Despite his promise of complete secrecy, Alex fleshed out what Santo had said to him, from the involvement of the CIA to the Guatemalan training camp. If he was to receive a meaningful judgment from Meyer, his friend needed all the facts at his disposal.

"Alex, I can't pretend that I wouldn't benefit from Cuba opening up to US tourism again, although, with a different leader in charge, we might not operate on quite the same terms."

"That only happens if the plan is successful. Do you think we have a good chance of whacking the old buzzard and should I be the one to do it?"

"Killing Castro shouldn't be that difficult if you spend time on the island and monitor his movements and routines. The chances are that he'll have grown complacent. The bigger issue is whether you'd be able to get away after the deed is done. We both saw first-hand how loyal his people are to him. They are unlikely to let us go to the airport and take the first plane home."

"Meyer, if it was me going through the streets of Havana, I'd believe I had a very good chance of a lucky sniper shot piercing his skull. Santo and the CIA appear to have got themselves a small army. I can lead the men, but Castro's execution will be that much harder with a squad under my command."

"Remind me again why Santo wants the hit?"

"It's come from Kennedy."

"Sure. Right…"

IN THE MORNING, Alex sat with Lansky in the dining room and they consumed yet another pot of coffee.

"All these deals boil down to trust, Alex. You know that, right?"

"Yes, Meyer. My attitude to the Italians differs from yours. Santo and I have got along just fine over the years."

"When you do business with one, you do business with them all. You might think Santo is a good fella, but can you say the same of the rest of the mob bosses, even the ones you haven't met?"

"Of course I can't, but does that mean I shouldn't touch the hit? If you felt this strongly then why did you launder mafia money for so long?"

"Sometimes two people have an alignment of interests. When you walk along the same sidewalk as another fella, then you both have a vested interest in ensuring that the path ahead is smooth because neither of you wants to trip up. After a length of time, interests diverge and then you are walking on your own and no one is looking after your back."

"And, Meyer, I suppose in Cuba you both were on the same path?"

"I wanted cash flow, and he needed clean gelt, but now we are both in Florida and I no longer have a series of casinos to launder his Vegas skim. Do I get a call from Santo? No, I do not. Instead, you hear his voice on the line and he flies you over to hire you to kill Fidel Castro."

Meyer stirred his coffee without purpose, as he had added neither sugar nor cream. Alex pondered for a second.

"By that reasoning, Santo and I should do fine. He wants the guy dead to keep Kennedy happy and to reopen Cuba to US investment. I want the money Santo will pay me."

"You have forgotten to factor in the CIA, Alex."

"When the mob and the CIA work together, the government agents can't do anything about any of our other business enterprises because we'd have no reason to keep our mouths shut. Imagine what the papers would say if they found out a president had hired organized crime bosses to murder Castro."

"Alex, I see the alignment of interest between you, Santo, and the CIA handler keeping the matter silent, but is that enough for you to work together to hit Castro?"

"What else do you think we need, Meyer? We would all be looking for the death of the man who stole our property and chased us out of the country."

"Alex, that is a connection between you and the Italian. My question was whether you trusted the CIA."

Alex thought for a minute.

"They will only do what Kennedy tells them to do. No more and no less."

"Are you implying that you trust Kennedy? I mean, he has been good to Israel, I agree, but I'm not sure that means he'd always have your back, no matter what."

"Meyer, if that was all there was between Jack and me then you'd be right."

"What ace do you hold up your sleeve?"

"I supply narcotics to the president of the free world when he flies into California to see his girlfriends. And a shell company set up by David and Moishe has won state construction contracts. We have an arrangement so that some federal contracts will head my way too."

Now it was Meyer's turn to sink into somber thought.

"What *chutzpah*. You are walking a dangerous tightrope, my friend."

"He has been feeding me contracts since we returned to the US, so I wouldn't say I trust him. He is a politician, but there is an alignment of interest. We walk on the same sidewalk; he wants my silence and I want his contracts."

"Alex, we have waited all our lives for a president in our pocket and you moved to the other side of the country and picked one up along the way."

"You take what you can find."

"That leaves us with the Italians, then."

"I think they are there for the ride because of Santo's history in Cuba. The CIA could rustle up some soldiers, a few Marines, and enough air power to blast the hell out of the island."

"So, Alex, why do you need him at all? Why not make the same deal direct with Kennedy and cut out Santo as the middleman?"

"If I do that, then I will create an enemy out of Santo and there is no need to create unnecessary foes in this life."

"I've told you before, you cannot trust Trafficante. Were you invited to the Appalachian conference?"

"No, Meyer."

"Because they don't want Jews at the top table. If there are any problems, then Santo will turn his back on you at the earliest opportunity."

"The gelt will help me retire and look after my family for the remainder of their lives."

"Look around, Alex. What little money I salvaged from Cuba is in the bricks of this house. Do I have cash coming out of my ears? I do not, but I can still spend the rest of my days in quiet comfort. If you have any sense, then you should do the same as me and save yourself all the *tsoris*."

9

ALEX PLANNED TO spend a week with Sarah as he wasn't sure when he would see her again. Despite Meyer's protestations, the lure of Santo's money was too great.

"Must you put your life on the line just for the sake of a bag of cash, Alex?"

"Tomorrow is always difficult to predict and I need to be certain you will be well provided for, no matter what happens to me."

"Don't talk like that, Alex. You sound as though you have a death wish."

"I have no desire to die, Sarah, but at some point, I shall. Until then, I plan to stay alive as long as I am able and that means I must make provision for you so that when I am gone, you need worry for nothing."

"If this is just another hit, then why won't you tell me what you are going to do? Your reticence makes me feel as though you are involved in something far more dangerous. Tell me I'm wrong."

"Let's enjoy the next few days together, Sarah, and let the future unfold before us at its own pace."

Alex stepped onto the patio carrying a pot of coffee to lure Sarah from the dining room. She shrugged and followed him out, perching herself on the edge of a sunbed. In contrast, he lay down and shut his eyes for a spell. A minute later, she relented and copied him until they both soaked in the warmth of the afternoon sun.

◆ ◆ ◆

ALEX'S FIRST STOP was to Useppa Island, just west of Lee County in Florida. The place used to be a resort, but the last hotel had closed its doors a year or two back. Manuel Artime, a Cuban national, met him at the pier and showed him around the small-town buildings.

"Manuel, thank you for the tour, but what are you doing here?"

"Alex, I taught at the Havana military academy after the fall of Batista, but soon I realized that the revolution was being thwarted by the leadership."

"Castro, you mean?"

"Let's just say I needed to leave Cuba in a hurry and here I am working with some of our mutual friends to rid my country of the vermin who are turning it into a rotten state."

"Castro has a lot to answer for. I'd be happy to see the back of him and return to Havana."

"What did you do there, Alex?"

"I was involved in the entertainment industry."

"Singer?"

"Not quite, but I knew a few. I helped to run a hotel or two."
Manuel stiffened.

"So, Alex, you'd like the country to return to its capitalist ways?"

"I don't believe in revolution if that is what you are asking, but I want a change of government over there. Our interests are aligned and that should be sufficient. If we are successful, then we can argue about what sort of state Uncle Sam allows later on."

Artime walked Alex over to a ramshackle hotel. There was no one still living who could remember its glory days. The Cuban introduced him to Elías, Paquito, and Juanfran, who had been recruited by a guy called Gerry Drecher.

"Paquito, are you hoping for a new dawn once we remove Castro from his people's throne?"

"For sure. I want to get back to my import/export business."

"How about you, Elías?"

"If I were in charge, then I'd call General Batista to be president again."

"Me too," added Juanfran.

The conversation flowed for another five minutes and then Alex decided he wanted to rest in his room for a while. Manuel showed him his second-floor quarters and Alex invited him inside.

"You appear to be the only revolutionary. Is every other member of the crew seeking to reinstate Batista?"

"Depends who recruits them. I want a new nirvana; Drecher is less choosy."

"When do you expect that I'll meet him?"

"Tomorrow maybe, or the day after. He is due back soon."

"You know much about him?"

"Nothing. He recruited me, sent me to this island, and spends his time on trips to Miami, finding disaffected Cubans to join our group. Then he goes back and repeats the process. Just one thing, what is your role here? Gerry told me you'd be arriving but gave me no idea why you were joining the fight."

"I am here to run the show. You can direct the men as much as you want, but we will all be executing my plan, once I've figured out what it is."

"We had better find you a uniform."

"When I left the army, I was only a private, and that was a long time ago."

"Well, you're a general in Brigade 2506 now. Congratulations on your promotion, sir."

GERRY ARRIVED ON the island two days later and Alex seized the chance to meet him before he scurried back to Miami. He checked into Alex's hotel so they could have lunch together with no effort.

"Good to see you in the flesh. Everyone talks about you in hushed awe. You are the guy from the CIA and that is the only thing people know about you."

"Alex, that is how it will stay. I turn up, I do my job, and then I leave. The rest doesn't matter."

"Gerry, if that's your real name, how well do you know Cuba?"

"I've stared at enough maps to be comfortable with the terrain."

"Ever visited? Even as a tourist?"

"That would be classified, Alex."

"No, it wouldn't. You might believe you aren't authorized to talk about clandestine jobs Uncle Sam has sent you on, but if you went somewhere on vacation, then that is fair game for our conversation. Gerry, have I been recruited just because I have driven on some of the roads?"

"Not entirely, but it sure does help us. Almost all the men are Cuban, so they'll know every nook and cranny of the island. From what I've heard from our mutual friends, you have the experience of fleeing the country while being chased by Castro's forces at the airport."

"Are you talking about Santo or somebody else?"

"Now, that is classified."

A broad grin swept across Gerry Drecher's face and he chuckled.

"I shall need to bring in some of my own people, Gerry."

"Show me a list of names and I will vet them. When I give the go-ahead, then you can contact them."

"That is not the way it is going to be, Gerry. If the two fellas aren't with me, then the deal is off and the brigade can kill Castro without me."

The grin flung itself onto the floor and Drecher stared at Alex, who lit a cigarette to give the man time to reach a decision.

"I must insist, Alex."

"No, you don't. Let's just say that they do not need the level of scrutiny from the US government that your background check will entail."

"What makes you think we didn't do the same with you?"

"Gerry, my invitation to join this party did not come from the CIA or any government agency. In case you are unaware, Santo Trafficante asked me to assassinate Castro, and I agreed as a favor to him and other interested parties far more senior than you can imagine. I want Ezra Kohut and Massimo Sciarra or I'll take the next ferry back to the mainland."

"Alex, can we trust them?"

"I have trusted my life and the lives of my family members to them more times than I can remember. They need no CIA authorization, as I have known them for over forty years. If I couldn't rely on them for anything I may ask, I would have put a bullet in their skulls decades ago."

Gerry considered his response.

"Let me make a call and confirm they can join the brigade without formal vetting by my department."

"That's fine. I understand you have protocols with which you must comply. Only don't mention them by name. I want no record of their involvement in this project, apart from their salaries. Tell your superiors they will receive half the amount I am being paid. Take it or leave it."

"I like you already, Alex. No messing about, a man after my own heart."

With the main order of business out of the way, the two men ate their buffet lunch. As Alex mopped up the pasta sauce from his bowl, he dragged the conversation back to the brigade Gerry was forming.

"I understand why you'd want the likes of Artime in the brigade, but why fill the ranks with Batista supporters? He did nothing for the country except bleed it dry."

"Alex, if the guy is anti-Castro, then that is good enough for me. What happens after we remove Fidel is not my concern. We shall create the power vacuum and somebody else, with way more stripes than I possess, will choose the next Cuban leader."

"And open up the place for American tourists?"

"In an ideal world, why not?"

10

WITHIN TWO DAYS, Ezra and Massimo arrived in Florida, and Alex picked them up from the airport. They were stationed in rooms on either side of his, which meant they could spend time together, away from the other men. All three helped Gerry whip the brigade into shape through a mix of PT and classroom sessions on war strategy.

Most of the guys who had signed up to the show knew a trade, but some were professionals: doctors, lawyers, accountants. They picked up the war games quicker than the rest and were destined to join the officers, but they were klutzes, almost to a man.

"Gerry, we need fighters, and the guys we have who want to see Batista reinstated are not much to work with. They'll get killed before we jump out of the plane."

"Alex, you worry too much. This is only the first stage of their training. By the time my men have worked with them, this raw material will be transformed into something brilliant."

Alex was not convinced and he could tell by Ezra's and Massimo's expressions that they shared his concerns.

"We are leading these guys into slaughter. If you are serious about toppling Castro, we are going to need more than this bunch to achieve it. I remember seeing the hate in the peasants' eyes, and that was before the revolution began."

"Ezra is right. Americans were spat on in the street. Gerry, you underestimate the size of the task at hand."

"Alex, you seem to think we do not already have assets on the ground. The Company has more than one plan underway for Operation Mongoose."

"Are you telling me you have agents on the island and you still need us to swan over and take him out? Why not use those fellas to do the job?"

"An intelligence officer is not the best person to carry out an assassination, Alex."

Massimo cleared his throat. The fella generally let others talk and he listened, but not today. "We are missing the point here. Just because you have found some Cuban exiles who want to see the end of Castro does not mean we can train them well enough to cope with a military attack. Gerry, you need to rethink your plans."

The CIA operative inhaled. "You are not listening to me. We have put in place several initiatives, all of which are geared around killing Castro. By the time we head for Cuba, this ragtag band of brothers will be a well-oiled fighting machine. It is our job to all make certain that is the case. When we move to the second camp, then we shall introduce you to our other assets who will work on these men until they come up to the mark."

Alex finished his coffee and lit a cigarette. These CIA guys were sure of themselves, but Gerry had done nothing to show why he should be so certain of his abilities.

THEIR MILITARY PLANE touched down in Guatemala three days later. It had not been a comfortable journey, especially when compared to the private jet Alex had enjoyed before, but they were safe and installed in their barracks within hours of arriving in the country.

"Do you think the men are prepared enough, Alex?"

"Ezra, they'd be lucky to take over a local bar and get a free drink."

"Gerry stores a lot of faith in the CIA training."

"I overheard him say they had the go-ahead for the invasion, so it can't be long now."

"Massimo, keep your ears close to the ground. It sounds as though Gerry wants to keep us in the dark."

The three men stood watching the brigade as it mustered for morning reveille. There may have been thirty-five men who had come over with them from Florida, but Alex counted almost thirteen hundred in front of him. If he had believed this was going to be a small sortie, with him at the helm sneaking into Castro's quarters, then the sheer scale of the army before him showed he was mistaken.

"Would our mission not be better served if we made a clandestine landing and positioned a sniper in a well-located building, Gerry?"

"We considered that option and decided against it as that puts all our eggs in one basket. With this many men, we have a stronger chance of getting at least one guy into the center of Havana and putting a bullet in Castro's brain."

"You are setting us up for a bloodbath. Even to land all these guys is going to take a miracle."

"Alex, that is the easy bit. We can send them onto the beach under cover of night. As you know, there are many weaknesses in the island defenses and insufficient troops to maintain patrols at every piece of the coastline."

"Gerry, do you have any concrete plans to reach Castro?"

"You will lead the advance party to find the best routes to Havana and feed that back to the brigade. Some of them will spread out across the country to cause as much confusion as possible and to mask who is aiming for the primary target."

"So no actual idea how to kill the guy apart from throwing a thousand men onto the island and hope that someone gets lucky."

"Alex, we are shipping over enough troops so that Castro's forces will have no knowledge that you and your friends are going to assassinate Castro. Everything else is window dressing."

Alex pondered the proposal before him.

"That still sounds mighty thin to me, especially as I am the one who'll be in the thick of it, while you'll relax, smoking a stogie back here or in Florida."

"I'm not a cigar man, Alex, but you do not need to be concerned. I have seen my fair share of action over the years."

"But I am right? You're not joining us for this trip, are you?"

"No, Alex. I will sit this one out."

"Gerry, we need longer. First, I require a much more detailed and well-thought-out plan of attack. Second, we call them men, but they are nothing but a bunch of intellectuals and store owners. These guys are far from being a fighting force we can rely on. We must have a few more weeks to train them into something useful."

"Time is one commodity we have little of. With my current budget, I could buy each of us a top-flight hooker and still have enough money left to arm everyone twice over. But the launch date remains fixed."

"When are we aiming for?"

"Come hell or high water, we sail on April seventeenth."

Alex sighed and let out a long whistle through the gap between his front two upper teeth. Ezra and Massimo shifted in their seats to indicate their disquiet with the situation Gerry was presenting to them.

"What's the rush?"

"We still have a week, Alex, but there are other factors at play, so the date is set and cannot be changed. Besides, there'll be no moon, which should make the first few hours of the assault easier, especially if you are right and these guys are going to end up as cannon fodder."

Gerry indicated the sea of Cuban exiles in front of them, and Alex shuddered. The memory of leaping out of trenches into no man's land amid a hail of shells and shrapnel ripped across his mind. Then he snapped away from France and back to reality.

"We need more time, Gerry."

"Ask for boats, bullets, planes, or guns and I can get them all in less than twenty-four hours with one phone call, but we can't extend the assault by even a day."

"Why?"

"That's above my pay grade, Alex."

"You are sending these men to a certain death, Gerry."

"In which case, it is your duty to save them. The sooner you get to Castro, the quicker this thing ends."

"The only way it'll work is if I am in the reconnaissance party."

"Whatever it takes to get the job done, Alex. Succeed, and the world is your oyster."

11

TWO DAYS BEFORE they were due to attack what they hoped would be the soft underbelly of Cuba, Alex ran through the plan once again with Ezra and Massimo.

"We lead the three flotillas so that they land half a mile apart. Once we hit the beaches, the enemy will be spread thin along the south coast."

"Alex, Massimo, and I think we need to rearrange matters. We are not happy about you being in the firing line. You should be somewhere less… risky."

"Ezra, I can look after myself. You two are not responsible for my safety."

"Alex, we want you to be alive at the end of the operation. You make your own choices, but Gerry doesn't have to drag you home in a body bag."

"Massimo, I'll be fine. Of the three of us, you should remember that I am the only one to have fought in a war."

Both men looked at each other, and Alex knew they didn't believe his bravado. Gerry had promised him he would arrange air cover from the time they landed until he radioed to say they were pushing through into the foothills.

"You fellas worry too much. This isn't some flight of fancy, we have the CIA watching our backs. Can you imagine that? The US government is riding shotgun on this trip."

"Remind me where Gerry is going to be when we land, Alex."

"Ezra, you know he is coordinating all activities from a gunship."

"So, he won't put his ass on the line then?"

Alex sighed. "No, but we are the ones who are getting paid the big bucks, and all he gets is a service pension."

THERE HAD ONLY been two occasions in his past that Alex had sat in a boat as small as the one he found himself in now. The first time was arriving on a French beach during the Great War and the second was at the start of Prohibition when Arnold Rothstein funded trips from Europe to deliver Scotch to the high-end clientele who could afford the luxury of imported liquor. As the waves lapped far too close to his head for comfort, Alex's thoughts were more focused on his old khakis than when he discovered the taste of whisky.

Ten other men clung on for dear life as their small vessel bobbed and weaved its way toward the Cuban shore. Alex squinted into the semidarkness, wondering how much longer they were going to be stuck in this floating coffin. He received his answer within two minutes when a whisper ran across the lips of every person on the craft. "Land."

He braced himself because he knew what would happen next. Everybody lurched forward as the hull hit the sand with a thud and the boat ground to a halt, listing to one side. The men needed no instruction as they leaped out into the water and scurried for dry land. Alex thought he heard gunfire in the distance and wondered if it was his imagination or if Ezra's and Massimo's flotillas had arrived first and were meeting some resistance.

There was no time to ponder because a hail of bullets ripped into the sand on either side of his feet. Everybody zigzagged toward the tree line, rifles in hand, and Alex did his best to look ahead to spot flashes from gun barrels so he could figure out where the enemy was located.

The trees seemed far away with bullets zinging past his ears, but three hundred feet and a lifetime later, Alex reached the foliage and hunkered down. There was still no sign of where Castro's forces were hidden. He popped his eyes above the bush in which he was hiding and counted heads. Three dead in the first five minutes.

Alex's biggest concern was that whoever was trying to pin them down would radio headquarters to tell them what was happening. His advance party would be the sum total of the invasion if that were to happen.

Then a whistle and Cecilio Guadarrama indicated he had something to show. A finger pointed toward a mound one hundred feet from where they were on the edge of the tree line. Alex nodded and gestured for everyone to stay put. He circled around the trees on his hands and knees until he was only fifty feet away and saw the whites of a sixteen-year-old's eyes. A single crack rang out and he thought about how men still sent children into battle.

Silence. Alex waited a minute before doing anything else and when he was certain they were alone on the waterfront, he signaled out to sea to let the ship know it was safe to send the troops and tanks on shore. With a handful of boats and a shallow beach, landing the whole army was going to take hours to complete and Alex's job was to ensure that his seven men stayed alive long enough to deal with any interference the local militia might throw at them.

For now, there was nothing to do but lie and wait, although Cecilio reported that Ezra and Massimo were under fire.

"Where is their air cover? Gerry told us they'd attacked the airfields yesterday and that the Air Force would continue its bombardment throughout today and tomorrow."

"No idea, but it doesn't look like we've any protection from the skies."

"GET ME EZRA on the line, Cecilio."

Alex waited for his radioman to raise his lieutenant.

"How are you doing, Ezra?"

"We are fine, at least for now. We have been under fire from the moment we landed, but we've hunkered down in positions near the tree line. And you?"

"There was not much opposition when we arrived, although it's heated up overnight."

"I thought Gerry promised air cover."

"Words are cheap, Ezra. Since when did we trust G-men?"

"After they asked us to assassinate Fidel Castro, Alex."

They both chuckled.

"Back to the militia, Ezra. You said they met you as you hit the beach?"

"Yeah, it was like they knew we were coming."

"Well, the Air Force hammered the airport and other military outposts the day before, so you don't have to be a tactical genius to realize that something was about to happen."

"Alex, I hadn't thought about it that way. You're correct. Have I mentioned the lack of support?"

"Let it go, Ezra. You are right, but it will not make a difference. For whatever reason, the bombers have flown back home. We won't be seeing them again."

"Do you think we have a chance in hell of getting to Castro, Alex?"

"I don't know, to be honest. Unless Massimo has broken through and is heading for Havana as we speak, I can't see how we are going to overcome all these militias."

"I spoke with him just before we talked. They landed tanks with his men and have made some headway. He plans to hightail it to the airstrip at Giron and use that as a base."

"If you and I make it off the beach, then we should head for the hills. From there we can wage guerrilla warfare on Castro, just like he did to Batista when the roles were reversed."

"I hear you, Alex, but I don't know how successful I'll be at reaching the foothills. Our positions are safe for the moment, but if the locals get any kind of reinforcement..."

Alex's throat felt dry, and he tried to conjure saliva in his mouth.

"Ezra, if you have the choice between encroaching into Castro's territory or living to tell the tale to your grandchildren, make sure you get back home. No matter what. Cuba's freedom isn't worth dying for."

"Straight back at you, Alex."

FOUR HOURS LATER and Alex's men had dug into positions on the far side of the woods to give cover for the main force behind them as it landed and attempted to make some headway inland. The lookout gave a whistle to indicate troops were coming their way. Ten more minutes and bullets flew past his head and peppered the bodies of two more of his special squad.

"Get word to the beach, Cecilio. Either they send men to support us or we'll have to pull back to the shore."

"Our instructions just in are to retreat, Alex."

"Then what are we doing still talking?"

Alex issued the order and the five men withdrew until there was sand under their feet and not soil. Still the bullets zipped past. The Cuban militia was advancing and there was no time to hang around. The brigade opened fire on Castro's militiamen as soon as they appeared through the trees and Alex's crew zigzagged back along the beach and onto one of the small boats which had disgorged men onshore only a minute before.

"Take me the hell off this island."

The instruction tore out of his throat and the boatman blinked and followed his orders to the letter.

12

"I AM SO happy to see you."

Alex's sister, Esther, gave him an enormous bear hug, while two of his sons, Moishe and David, looked on. After a long weekend recuperating with Sarah from his Cuban escapade, Alex felt a powerful urge to see the rest of his family.

He walked into their New York office without announcing his arrival because he just wanted to meet them with no fanfares or anything fancy. A firm handshake for the boys and a pat on the shoulder each was the most Alex offered for physical affection, but the smile on his face spoke volumes.

"Aren't you glad you're no longer living in Cuba what with all that's been happening over there last week?"

Alex nodded at Esther, but David's expression showed the lawyer guessed there was much more to reveal.

"How is Mom? And how are Ezra and Massimo?"

"She is fine and enjoying Californian life… and they got out by the skin of their teeth."

"Huh?" Esther was naïve but Moishe figured his father had been involved.

"It's been a long time since you've been this side of the country, Pop."

"Moishe, I can't tell you how busy I have been, but it is great to be here with you all now."

"Did you try a mojito before you left?"

"Don't get fresh, David. Whatever you may think, I will not comment. Just be pleased that Ezra and Massimo made their way to an airstrip by a whisker and escaped. From what I read in the newspaper, there's a thousand or more captured by Castro's forces."

"Like I said, Alex. I am so glad that your Havana jaunt is behind you," Esther reiterated.

THAT NIGHT, ALEX hosted a meal in a private dining room at the Waldorf-Astoria on the strict understanding that Lindy's cheesecake would be procured for dessert. The dinner went with a swing, and then they hopped over to Broadway to catch a show. Esther was in her element and couldn't stop squeezing Alex's arm to call attention every time there was some item of note that she had spotted.

David and Moishe were more relaxed about the stars they saw on stage, in part because so many American hoofers had visited Cuban hotels during their time in Havana. Once the performance was over, David suggested a nightcap before they headed home.

Alex's eyes shifted from David to Esther and back, but his son nodded with a gentle smile. She might have left Cuba with a liquor problem, but she could enter a drinking establishment without falling apart. In the Waldorf bar, the three men ordered Scotch, and she asked for a soda and lime, much to Alex's relief.

Conversation twisted and turned for an hour as everyone sipped their drinks, not wanting to finish the evening too soon. Chuckles and stories abounded as Alex caught up on everyone's lives. He did his best not to talk about work because he had no desire to open himself up to the old discussion about how much he should let his sons know about the less reputable side of his business empire. David especially had grabbed a glimpse and might have been in awe of the powerful people in Alex's sway, but the boy was not ready to handle himself in the criminal world that Alex called home.

Esther's eyes began to droop, and Alex suggested he call her a cab, which she accepted without question. They walked through the lobby and out to the front of the building to wait for a hotel porter to hail a taxi.

"It's been great to spend time with you today, Alex. You haven't said how long you are in town for."

"That's because I don't know yet, Esther. At least a couple of days, maybe longer. While the focal point of the trip is to see you guys, there are one or two errands I need to take care of."

"There always is with you, Alex."

She winked at him, and then pecked him on the cheek as the porter opened the passenger door of the yellow cab. Alex took care of the guy, and Esther zoomed off into the night.

Hands in pockets, Alex sauntered back to his sons, who had ordered another round of drinks.

"Hope you didn't mind, Pop, but we don't like to let Aunt Esther see us with too much liquor."

"What's to mind?"

They clinked glasses and Alex called for three stogies to be delivered to the table.

THE FOLLOWING MORNING, Alex returned to the Cohen office and talked business with all three of his employees. Esther handled the day-to-day smooth running of the company that Alex had set up to keep her busy once she'd wrestled herself out of a tequila bottle after her return from Cuba. Legal advice came from David and as Moishe was a trained accountant, he was the go-to guy where financial matters were concerned.

"How's the Vegas cash flow, Esther?"

"There's been a dip in the last month. When I called Massimo and then Ezra, they were missing. I asked around, but nobody had a clue where they were."

"With me. We were investigating a new investment opportunity."

"Any good?"

"The entire deal fell through, more's the pity."

"So we can expect your eyes and ears in Las Vegas to be on top of things again?"

"Yes. Let me know if a shortfall in May is likely. Tell me by the end of the first full week. Those two should be able to sort everything out by then and, if not, we will need to hatch a plan."

"Understood, Alex."

Then it was Moishe's turn to join Alex in the meeting room. Alex would have been happier conducting these conversations at the back of a nearby deli, but he hadn't been in town long enough to find a suitable location with a disinterested proprietor.

"Pop, I know you sent me away from Cuba, and I understand your reasons. In hindsight, it was an excellent thing for me."

"You're welcome, Moishe."

"But that doesn't mean I don't want more."

"My boy, has there ever been a moment in your life when that has not been the case?"

"Do not tease me, Pop. I am serious. You have kept me out of harm's way and protected me from whatever it is that earns you all your money. But I could do so much more for you if you let me."

"There is a reason I do not want you too involved in some of my affairs. If you have no clue where my gelt comes from, then you have plausible deniability if Uncle Sam were to come sniffing around into my finances again."

"This isn't about plausible deniability but that you exclude me from too many things. Imagine what I could do for you if you let me inside the circle of trust."

Alex raised his eyebrows.

"Moishe, just because I do not offer you full financial disclosure, please don't mistake that for a lack of confidence in you on my part. Quite the reverse. It is because I know you and believe in your strong moral compass that I trust you with my money, and the future of my family which provides me with the peace of mind I need to know that Sarah will never want for anything ever in her life. Knowing what you do, if you weren't in the circle of trust, then you would never have left Havana alive."

His son swallowed hard and remained silent. Alex lit another cigarette and sipped a mug of coffee, poured from the pot which Esther had made the minute he arrived that morning.

"Moishe, when the time is right, then I will rely on you to tend to all my finances, irrespective of their source. I hope to retire someday soon and then all my cash must be clean as your conscience. Until then, find comfort in knowing that you are one of the chosen few."

ONCE MOISHE HAD left the room, Alex placed a few calls and spoke with Sarah.

"How are you doing?"

"Missing you, Alex, but I pretend I am used to your absences."

"Please don't be like that, Sarah. Everyone here is giving me tsoris. Not you as well."

"You were back for such a short time before you went off again."

"Sarah, I needed to check on the family business. Besides, there are some acquaintances I need to meet. While we might not live in the pockets of the Italians, we still must feed and water their concerns."

David was the last to speak with Alex.

"How goes it, Pop?"

"Your mother wants me to come back home."

"Not before we've had a chat, I hope."

"David, that's the second time you've been fresh with me in the same number of days. Have I annoyed you?"

"Ever since we fled Cuba, I feel you've pushed me away."

Alex stared into David's eyes until he made his son uncomfortable.

"I made a mistake with the Cuban businesses and that was to give you too much insight into how I make my money. It put you in jeopardy, especially with our Italian friends, and I do not want to repeat that error now we are back in America."

"We all know how you earn a living, Pop. I've told you before that Moishe and I made our peace with that many years ago."

"Your Aunt Esther is less certain."

"She tells herself that your investments generate cash flow, and she doesn't for a minute wish to think how that gelt gets generated. What little she saw of you in Havana was enough for a lifetime."

"David, there is another reason I don't want you to be too close to my current activities, you need plausible deniability if Uncle Sam were to pay a visit."

13

ALEX SAT IN an anteroom, smoking a cigarette while he waited to be allowed in to discuss business with Joe Bananas. So far, he had been stuck in the chair for around ten minutes, but who was counting? A short while later, a door opened, and a fella in a suit beckoned him inside.

"Alex, I apologize for making you wait so long."

"Don't mention it. I was pleased you could find time in your day to see me."

Joe indicated for Alex to sit on a couch away from the man's desk. His underling supplied coffee and then left them alone. Alex lit yet another cigarette while he waited for the stooge to go.

"How's business, Joe?"

"I can't complain. You know how it is, if it's not one thing, then it is another, but we get by."

Alex cast an eye around Joe's office and noticed the gold leaf corners on the picture frames, the sheer acreage of the room itself, and the feel of the leather upholstery in his seat.

"Life on the commission must be tough. I rescinded my syndicate membership when people stopped coming to the meetings."

Joe curled the corners of his mouth and sipped his coffee.

"Some of my predecessors should have had the decency to tell you that the days of the syndicate were over."

"Kind of you to say so, Joe. I guess the Appalachian meeting was the nail in that particular coffin."

"Sixty of us were arrested that day and Hoover discovered organized crime for the first time in his life."

Alex thought how wrong Joe was. The Italians were grabbed by the Feds as no Jew was invited to the party.

"Water under the bridge, Joe. I try to look at the future. Do you have any interests on the West Coast?"

"Alex, now why do you ask me that?"

"Forgive my abruptness, Joe. I don't mix in the same circles as you do anymore. Let me explain. I have business in California and hope to expand my activities. However, the last thing I want to do is to lock horns with any person of influence as I grow."

"Do not undersell yourself, Alex. You might not sit at the top table with the Italian families, but you are known and respected. After all, if you were just the small-town operator you claim to be, then you would not be sitting here enjoying our conversation."

"Very kind, Joe. And you are right to say that I have worked with the Italian families over the years, here and overseas."

"Cuba was a tremendous opportunity for us all, Alex. How is Meyer these days?"

"Happy in Florida, from what I hear. I don't see him as much as I used to, besides he's retired and I'm still treading the boards."

"Retired, Alex? That's not the Meyer Lansky I know. That man always has some scheme cooking in the background."

"He told me he lost everything when Castro nationalized the casinos."

Joe smirked and shook his head. "Meyer's not down to his last nickel and dime just yet."

Was Joe jerking him around or had Meyer escaped with more than Alex realized? He had no method of figuring it out at the minute.

"Either way, Joe, you didn't answer my question."

"No? My apologies. Tough business in Cuba. Wouldn't you say?"

"It sure was..."

Alex's voice drifted away as he recalled the terror in the pit of his stomach on the Playa Giron, which then hopped his mind over to France fifty years before.

"Thank you for trying, Alex."

"You're welcome."

He responded on autopilot before he registered the implication of Joe Banana's comment.

"I mean, I'm always interested in finding profitable opportunities with exceptional business partners."

"No need to be coy, Alex. We all appreciate your efforts in returning Cuba to a sensible footing. It's just a shame things didn't work out for us."

"Some you win, Joe, some you lose."

"And that one, we sure lost."

Another sip of coffee, and Joe continued his line of thought.

"I find it interesting you inquire about the West Coast for two reasons. First, I assumed your territory for narcotics and prostitution was restricted to the Hollywood Hills and no further. Second, we are keeping a watchful eye on Frank."

"DeSimone?"

"For sure. The guy has run Los Angeles for six years now, but the area has never been secure for our interests since the days of Mickey Cohen and your friend Benny Siegel."

"Jack Dragna ruled with an iron fist."

"True, Alex, but you made inroads back then without too much opposition if I recall."

Alex smiled. Joe was well informed.

"Joe, if I were to expand my business, would that be problematic for you?"

"Not at all. If you can carve away more of Frank's empire, then you will hear no objection from me or any of the other families in New York. What do you have in mind?"

"Nothing in particular, but I wanted to ensure I wouldn't be stepping on your toes or conflicting with your interests when I make a move."

"Very considerate, Alex."

"We live together, we love together, but we die alone."

"Well said. Is there anything else you wanted to discuss?"

"Just one thing, Joe."

The man raised an eyebrow.

"My lieutenants have returned to Vegas, and I wondered if they should watch out for any issues you are aware of."

Joe stared at Alex without uttering a word.

"Are you on a fishing expedition, Alex? Because that sounded like the vaguest question I think I have ever heard. No disrespect."

"No sleight perceived, Joe. To be honest, I'm asking because it has been so long since I've been involved in the day-to-day Vegas casino operations. I thought I'd check that it remains an open city."

"Sure thing, Alex. Although everyone would like to have their own piece of Nevada, we allow it to remain neutral. Even nowadays."

"So the money should keep on rolling in?"

"If you carry on as you have been. I know I can speak for all five families when I say we continue to be happy with the way you help run the city. The casinos under your control continue to deliver their numbers and you have always been amenable to working with us over the years."

"Thank you, Joe. Ever since the Flamingo, I have done my best to generate money for all my partners in the casino business. Sometimes it hasn't been easy…"

"We all have our differences of opinion sometimes…"

"But I make as many accommodations as I am able. Vegas is an enormous pot of honey and if no one loses their head, then we can all enjoy its sweetness."

"Alex, you sound as though you are taking stock of your business empire."

"It's not quite an empire, not anymore at least. I have a few well-placed interests around the country and at some point, I want to retire."

"The racing wire, an iron grip on Vegas, access to the rich and famous, the ear of the president. These are no mere trifles, Alex. You are right that the days when you ran Manhattan have long since faded, but your influence in America is significant."

Alex felt the warmth in his cheeks.

"Thank you. I do my best. And I wouldn't say I have Jack's ear. We have a business relationship where I act as an agent between federal departments and some of our construction friends."

"Well put, Alex. I will not press you because I respect your privacy, but we both know that you have Kennedy's private line."

Alex did not respond and lit a cigarette instead.

"And on a separate note, Alex, I wonder if you'd be kind enough to get in touch with Sam Giancana over the next few days."

"Any particular reason beyond reminiscing about our time in Havana?"

"Alex, I'll leave Sam to run through the details, but I would see it as a personal favor if you were to do so. My understanding is that he'd like to talk to you about a mutual friend."

"We have picked up many of those over the years. Anyone, in particular, he has in mind?"

Joe Bananas sighed and sipped his coffee for the millionth time since they'd sat down.

"If you talk to Sam, then you'll find out. You don't need me to act as a broker. I'm just asking you for a favor."

"There's nobody else in the room. This is as far from a case of entrapment as you'll get. I'll just find it easier if I know who I'm going to be having a conversation about. Nothing more than that, Joe."

Another breath and a slug of coffee hit the back of Joe's throat.

"Frank Sinatra."

"A great singer, by all accounts. And can act too."

"He's brought plenty of customers to our casinos as well."

"Yeah, you could say that."

The two men smiled at each other and finished their coffees.

14

"HOW ARE YOU doing, Sam?"

"All the better for seeing you, Alex."

The two men shook hands and sat down in the back of a Chicago restaurant owned by Giancana.

"Fancy something to eat?"

"I'm good for now, but coffee would be wonderful. Joe sends his regards."

"It is kind of you to take time from your schedule to see me, Alex."

"Joe Bananas recommended we talk and here I am. He mentioned we had a mutual friend."

The waiter arrived with their drinks and they paused for the guy to be out of earshot before they continued.

"Frank has been very useful to us over the years. His turns in Vegas and Havana helped to encourage tourists into our hotels and casinos."

"We have both benefited from his performances, that's for sure."

"Alex, the thing is that he is hosting a weekend away for Kennedy and I'd like someone to be my eyes and ears when the two of them are together."

"Are you expecting any trouble?"

"Quite the reverse, Alex. My informants tell me that Jack Kennedy is tight with Frank, but Bobby Kennedy continues to obsess over mob involvement in American politics and industry. He's like a dog with a bone who refuses to spit it out. You'd be there to gauge the extent to which Bobby is influencing Jack. No more and no less."

"No disrespect, but why don't you visit instead of me?"

"Because I haven't met Kennedy and you have."

Alex thought for a minute and understood how he was better placed to assess the situation.

"Sam, how can I get an invitation?"

"I'll call Frank tomorrow and tell him he has an extra houseguest."

THE PALM SPRINGS home of Frank Sinatra was lavish even by that town's standards. Far from the city center, Frank's residence stood on two acres of grounds west of South Palm Canyon Drive. Sam had arranged a driver to collect Alex from the airport and fifteen minutes later they arrived at the main gates, where a guy in a peaked cap greeted Alex, then they drove on to the front of the house, away from any prying eyes from the street.

"Good to see you, Alex."

Frank welcomed him as soon as he stepped out of his limo.

"Straight back at you, Frank."

"Have you brought anything to help the house party go with a swing?"

"Don't you worry about a thing, Frank. I'll look after anyone who needs a little kicker."

Frank smiled and slapped Alex on the back then showed him around the enormous mansion he had built brick by brick to his own design. It was palatial, for sure, and there appeared to be sufficient staff to guarantee that every need would be met within seconds of it being thought. After Alex unpacked and came downstairs, Frank introduced him to his guests.

He recognized Peter Langford and Sammy Davis Jr. and met Dean Martin and Jerry Lewis for the first time. Everyone had brought a girlfriend along, and Alex wondered whether he should have got an invitation for Sarah. Then he checked himself because, unlike the others, he was here on business.

Jayne Mansfield swept into the living room and planted a kiss on Frank's lips, so Alex figured out who was his skirt for the weekend. Then two other men entered in quick succession: a young singer, Buddy Greco, and a comedian, Don Rickles. Everybody appeared to know each other and he wondered how well he would fit in and, therefore, how relaxed everyone would behave when Jack blew into town.

"Let me show you the helipad I had built for the presidential helicopter."

Frank took the group out of the back of the house, past the swimming pool, and then beyond the tennis courts, where a circular piece of tarmac had been plopped on top of a raised mound.

"We had to get foundations dug before the surface was laid. Those whirlybirds weigh a ton."

They all nodded and smiled. The men talked about construction for a short while and then their glasses needed to be refilled, so everyone sauntered to the booze at the rear of the house. Alex hung back to allow himself a few minutes' conversation away from the group.

"Thanks for letting me intrude on your weekend, Frank."

"All's good. Besides, when am I going to refuse Sam an accommodation? He wants you here, and why should I ask for any justification beyond that? Of course, that Peter's brother-in-law is due to land here in an hour might have something to do with it."

Sinatra winked at Alex but expected no response and none was forthcoming.

TWO HOURS LATER and no helicopter had landed. A further sixty minutes and still no bird had flown in from the sky. Frank's blue funk settled on him like a shroud, and even the close attention afforded by Jayne couldn't lift his mood. By this point, everyone had moved inside and Alex overheard a valet tell Sinatra that the dinner was well and truly burned. Nobody had wanted to eat before the president of the free world had arrived, which meant that at this rate, no one would eat at all.

Then a housekeeper popped her head around the door of the dining room and informed Frank that he had a telephone call. He stormed out and Alex followed him because the day was not going well and he wanted to keep a handle on the situation.

"Let me get this straight. Jack is staying with Bing Crosby tonight?"

The faint voice at the other end of the line responded, but Alex couldn't hear what was said.

"And when did you say he decided this?"

Muffled noise again and then Frank slammed the phone down, swearing in Italian for several seconds. Alex hung back, leaning against a door jamb. Sinatra stormed up and down his office until he had calmed down enough to be near his houseguests again.

"Jack will not be with us then, Frank?"

"No, Alex. He's staying with that Republican Crosby."

"Any idea why he changed his mind?"

"That rat-fink brother of his. Bobby told Jack he shouldn't be seen to mix with my sort anymore. That it's not acceptable for his image."

"Doesn't the attorney general like singers?"

Frank stared at Alex with an unimpressed expression.

"Let's just say the guy does not appreciate the entrepreneurial spirit, Alex."

"Do you think he understands how politics works?"

"Good question. From the moment the man uttered his first baby scream, he has lived inside the most political family in America. So you would expect he'd get the joke by now."

"Frank, I shall leave before breakfast tomorrow morning, but I might be back before the end of the weekend. Nothing personal, but without Jack here, I am going to be like some spare change and there is no need for me to make your guests feel uncomfortable."

"Alex, I appreciate your concern. Of course, you are always welcome in my home."

"JACK DIDN'T SHOW and stayed elsewhere that weekend."
Sam shook his head.

"The world we live in is very complicated. The Kennedys need to remember how they got into the White House."

Alex remained silent as Giancana continued.

"Let me guess. It was Bobby's decision and not Jack's? The president has always enjoyed hanging out with cool fellas like Frank. Bobby has a broom stuck up his ass, and he has a hard-on for organized crime."

Alex winced but did not respond until Sam had calmed himself down.

"Someone needs to do something about Bobby Kennedy."
Italian eyes pierced into Alex.

"Is that an instruction, Sam?"

"No, but thank you for the offer. I appreciate it."

"If you ever change your mind…"

Now it was Sam's turn to smile.

ALEX HOPPED OVER to Frank's Palm Springs mansion again the following week.

"What are you going to do about Bobby Kennedy?"

"Frank, as much as you want me to take action, I have not been authorized to do anything. And you must respect that decision."

Sinatra glared at Alex but chose not to follow up and changed the conversation to something more fun.

"Been to any parties the last few weeks?"

"Frank, you know Hollywood far better than me. Blink and there's another party to go to. Besides, you film stars like to have an entourage with pretty girls and plenty of narcotics."

"You've always been there for me and my gatherings."

"It's nice to help nice people."

They clinked glasses and settled in for a night of jokes and conversation.

"How does Jack get away with it, Frank?"

"What do you mean?"

"Well, the guy has at least two of Hollywood's biggest stars for girlfriends and somehow keeps both of them dangling on the line."

"Alex, everyone lives in denial. Marilyn and Jayne know about each other, but they tell themselves that the other is one of Jack's friends and nothing more. That way, they convince themselves they are his exclusive lover."

15

ALEX SETTLED BACK into his Hollywood routine with Sarah, supplying girls and drugs to any actor who had a credit on any movie that was on general release. Cannabis was the narcotic of choice although Alex noticed there had been an increasing call for coke over the past few months.

Sarah couldn't say there were any changes in the sexual tastes of their clients: teenage girls. It didn't matter the color of their skin or the shape of their hairstyle. If the skirt was short enough and the flesh willing, then they would do just fine. Alex never judged what any of his customers did with their money; that was their decision and their right. Sarah had a different perspective.

"Alex, do you ever imagine what would have happened to me if we hadn't got married?"

"What do you mean?"

"I'd still be in the old life."

"Sarah, after all these years? Do you think you'd have remained living the nafka life?"

"What are you trying to say?"

Alex was silent for half a second, and then he raised his eyebrows.

"That's not what I meant. You are still an amazingly attractive woman."

"Too little, too late, young man."

"I was attempting to tell you that you were too smart to work for Waxey Gordon for the rest of your life."

Sarah looked at him to consider his words, but her expression gave nothing away.

"Kind of you to say so, but Waxey Gordon only set me free after you paid him off. Without your gelt…"

Alex placed a hand on Sarah's arm and squeezed it.

"What's got you wondering about the maybes of our past?"

"Not much. With you back home, I was remembering how I felt when we first lived together when you returned to the Bowery after the war."

TWO DAYS LATER and Alex sat in an armchair in Marilyn Monroe's living room. A housekeeper had let him in and instructed he wait for her there. Ten minutes staring into space and Marilyn appeared in a figure-hugging powder blue dress. He smiled as she walked toward him.

"Sorry for making you wait, Alex."

"Don't mention it. I know how busy you actors are."

"No need for that tone, Alex."

"Only kidding."

She punched him on the arm but didn't even make a dent in his jacket.

"I've got a visitor arriving in a short while. Do you have what I asked for?"

Alex nodded, removed some folded brown paper from his coat pocket, and flicked it with his fingers.

"I think this is what you requested."

Now it was Marilyn's turn to smile, and she shimmied over to a sideboard. She opened a drawer and pulled out a small roll of notes, which she deposited in Alex's hand, with a kiss on the cheek as a bonus.

"Marilyn, is there anything else I can get you for your party tonight?"

"I said I'm expecting one visitor, not a gaggle of friends. Jack wouldn't appreciate coming all this way to share me with others."

That Kennedy sure knew how to keep his ladies happy, despite being president of the United States and having the first lady so much in the public eye.

"Marilyn, will I have time to go before Jack turns up?"

Before she could inhale to answer, the doorbell rang and thirty seconds later, Jack appeared in the living room, followed by the hapless housekeeper. The couple embraced, which gave Alex the excuse to leave the building. The only acknowledgment he received from Kennedy was a small nod before the president fondled Marilyn's ass.

JACK MUST HAVE been busy, because less than twenty-four hours later, Alex bumped into him again, only in Jayne Mansfield's home. His head popped round the doorway of her bedroom and Alex wondered if the two of them ever spent any time in the other rooms of her expansive house. Perhaps the decor was not as offensive as elsewhere, in which case Alex understood Jack's desire to be in Jayne Mansfield's boudoir; apart from the obvious reason, of course.

"Hi, Jack. How's it going?"

"Just fine, Alex."

Jayne pulled on the strings of her nightgown to tighten the front, but the sheer material left little to Alex's imagination and he clenched his teeth until the pressure on his molars became too intense. There was no need for her to behave that way. It felt as though she was playing games with Jack and was trying to place Alex in the middle. Jack's head disappeared from view and Alex was forced to talk business with Jayne.

"Is there anything else you require for your house party?"

"No, it looks like you've brought everything a girl could want for her man."

A wink and a coquettish smile. She padded over to a chest and opened the top drawer. Then she returned and placed both hands on either side of his and stared him square in the eyes.

"That's all for you."

For reasons beyond Alex's understanding, she planted a kiss on his cheek and he looked down to see the green Jayne'd pushed into his hand.

"Time for you to go back to Jack. Enjoy your night of passion. Call me any time if you need anything else."

Another smile and Jayne undid her nightgown to get it to slip on the floor as she turned around to walk into the bedroom.

"Come here, baby," were the only words Jack spoke before Alex trotted down the stairs and let himself out. Had Jayne left the door open for his benefit or because that's the way Jack liked it?

16

FOLLOWING A PHONE call from Jack a couple of weeks later, Alex drove down from Hollywood to Malibu and entered a swanky house on the beach itself. A butler greeted him on his arrival and led him through the building and out onto a patio.

Two men in black suits stood on the other side of a swimming pool with their backs to a summerhouse. Alex noted a pair of figures inside through the windows. A maid offered him a drink, and he accepted a coffee and waited.

Only when she returned and inquired if he wanted a refill, did the door to the summerhouse open and Jack appear. He waved at Alex and beckoned for him to come over.

"Good to see you, Alex. Have you met Bobby?"

The two men walked inside as Jack spoke and before Alex could answer, he was shaking hands with the attorney general. All three sat down in armchairs that surrounded a low table. Alex poured himself a cup from the coffeepot and settled into his seat.

"How's business, Mr. Kennedy?"

"Call me Bobby. The Department of Justice is doing just fine, thank you."

"Pleased to hear that federal law enforcement is protecting the citizenry from the evils of criminal enterprise."

"We do our best to remove all the vermin from our land, Alex."

He couldn't tell if Bobby had a way about him or whether those beady blue eyes were piercing into him especially, as though the brother knew about all of Alex's illegal business. He wondered how honest Jack had been about their relationship.

"Pest control is a wonderful thing, Bobby, and I am glad we have you on our side."

Now it was Bobby's turn to be silent for a moment as he judged Alex's comment.

"I saw that you have had your own trouble with the federal authorities."

Before Alex inhaled to reply, Jack stepped in. "That was long ago. He was a young man and served his time with dignity. We have all had youthful indiscretions."

Bobby scowled at his brother but chose not to continue the conversation. Alex took a sip of his coffee and waited to find out why he had been summoned here on such short notice. Just as Jack opened his mouth as if he was going to start a fresh discussion, he excused himself and left the summerhouse, and padded back to the main building. Alex looked at Bobby and smiled for half a second, but his expression was met with a scowl and a grimace.

"My brother is very forgiving, Alex."

"What do you mean by that, Bobby?"

"You are on record as a felon, like so many of your kind. Jack tolerates you but I do not."

Alex ground his molars. Whenever a *goy* talked of his kind, you could never tell if they meant other Jews or other criminals. Neither was good, but the former was far worse.

"I've paid for my past mistakes and my record has been clean ever since."

"That the authorities haven't indicted you for any crime in the last twenty years is not the same as saying that you have committed no felonies, Cohen. We both know that."

"Bobby, you should be careful about throwing casual accusations into a conversation. I am here because of my business relations with Jack. To cast aspersions on my activities is to do the same to your brother."

"The president is above reproach. You are not. Just remember that I am the attorney general and it is my job to root out all criminal activity in this country, organized or otherwise."

As Alex was about to respond, Jack returned and settled back in his armchair.

"What have you guys been talking about in my absence?"

"Bobby has been telling me of his plans to rid the country of organized crime."

"I'm going to exorcise all criminals from this fair land, Alex."

"A worthy aim, Bobby, and I applaud you but remember that not all business relationships are black and white. Most people operate in the fuzzy gray in the middle."

"You might, Alex. But the majority of hard-working Americans pay their taxes and follow the rules."

Alex allowed that comment to fall to the floor.

"So, Jack, why did you ask me to visit Malibu?"

"WHAT'S GOING ON, Alex?"

A blank expression met Sam Giancana's question.

"That Kennedy will be the death of me."

"Which one do you mean, Sam?"

"Bobby, of course."

Alex leaned back in his seat at the rear of the Miami restaurant where he and the mob boss were sharing coffee and cake.

"He is gunning for us, Sam. That's the simple truth and Jack doesn't appear to want to stop him."

"You just can't trust these people."

"Politicians are scum, have been since the glory days of Tammany Hall."

"And still are today, Alex."

"You said it, Sam."

"Is there anything specific we should be concerned about?"

"Not that I am aware of at present, Sam. Bobby talks the talk but he has done little in his fight against the high levels of the mob. So I think it is more about politics than actual plans. He wants to be seen to be doing the right thing, but he knows he'll end up implicating his brother if he digs too deep."

"We are going to need to do something about this family."

"Sam, what do you mean?"

The Italian sighed and took a swig of his coffee before guzzling half his tiramisu.

"Kennedy would never have moved into the White House if we had not offered our support. Our control of the unions and the influence we have over the Italian American community put him where he is today. And that man knows it."

"I wouldn't say Bobby acknowledged that with his behavior to me earlier this week."

"Alex, he agreed to turn a blind eye to some of our activities for the support we offered. He promised me that Bobby would do nothing to rock the apple cart."

"Then he was appointed attorney general."

"Yes. He got a taste for publicity when he was on a senate committee, but Hoover kept him in check. Now he is acting like he's ignoring what Jack has committed to."

"You know what we'd have done in the old days, Sam?"

A laugh.

"Yeah, but we live in a different age nowadays. I appreciate your offer, Alex. We shall let things slide for the moment. Unless Bobby uncovers any big deals, we can afford to allow a few opportunities to get exposed."

"There's also the minor fact that we are doing business with Jack, and Bobby will not want to besmirch the family name if it were to be revealed to the general public."

"They are both desperate for Joe Kennedy's attention. Their father keeps them under the thumb, and he and I worked together a long time ago."

"Sam, will that be enough to keep his boys in check?"

The mob boss weighed the question as he consumed the rest of his tiramisu.

"Let's just say that I am not impressed with Robert's ongoing actions and his implied threat when you met him. But I will watch and wait—for now at least."

ALEX STAYED IN town the next day so he could visit Meyer Lansky. Apart from an occasional phone call every month, the two men had little contact with each other. Alex told himself this was because of Meyer's retirement, but he was never sure that his old friend had stopped financing the mob's ventures.

"How are you doing?"

"All the better for seeing you, Alex."

Once they settled down in the living room and Thelma had left them alone, he cranked up the volume on the baseball match on the television.

"Meyer, I want your advice about Sam Giancana."

"What is that *schmendrick* up to now?"

"Let's just say we are having some issues with the Feds."

"Alex, you don't have to be circumspect with me. Whatever you say will go no further. No one calls, nobody visits."

"Sam has concerns about how far Bobby Kennedy will go in his desire to rid the country of organized crime."

Meyer smiled at the news.

"That family never ceases to amaze me."

"Meyer, are you going to suggest that Joe made his money out of bootlegging? That's what Sam implied to me."

"Don't be ridiculous. Joe's first fortune was generated by preparing well for the end of Prohibition. He sold legally imported booze as soon as the law changed."

"So why does Sam think he did business with Joe back then?"

"Maybe he did, but it had nothing to do with liquor, Alex."

"Meyer, how might I stop Sam from making a poor decision over Bobby?"

"I'm not sure you can, but I don't expect Sam will make any move on his own. The commission would need to authorize any significant action and I can't see that happening."

MAY 1962

17

ALEX SAT ON the far-left side of the auditorium at Madison Square Garden at a table containing a mix of Democrat faithful and interested businessmen. Sarah was next to him because they'd used the excuse of the fundraiser to hop over to New York to shop and relax with the family.

A single spotlight hovered in the middle of the stage as Peter Lawford introduced Marilyn Monroe for the umpteenth time that night. He'd set up a running gag that she was behind schedule.

"I introduce to you the late Marilyn Monroe."

The crowd laughed and Marilyn appeared in an ermine coat. The instant she removed it to reveal her skintight sequined dress, the audience clapped and cheered.

"Is she wearing anything underneath that thing?" Sarah whispered in Alex's ear and he shrugged in response. Then Monroe sang *Happy Birthday, Mr. President* to Jack, who was sat nearest the front.

As soon as the applause from the crowd had died down, a gigantic birthday cake was wheeled onto the stage and Jack joined her. Alex thought they made a strange couple and looked at Kennedy's table to see that his wife, Jackie, was nowhere to be found.

Once the show was over and every dime had been squeezed out of the assembled donors, Alex turned to Sarah.

"Now it's time for me to go to work at the after-party. I'll see you back at the hotel, but don't wait up. This could be a long night."

THE KENNEDYS AND senior Democrats were gathered in a library away from the main auditorium. A wall was lined with shelves stuffed to bursting with books. Alex took a drink offered by a waiter on his arrival and sauntered around the room to get his bearings.

One circuit later and Alex had spotted Jack and Bobby, along with Peter Lawford and Monroe. Bobby schmoozed some high rollers in one corner and Lawford chatted with Marilyn. A gaggle of senators and governors circled Jack, and everybody appeared to be laughing. Alex headed toward Marilyn with two glasses of champagne.

"Hello, Peter. Marilyn, what a performance tonight. Here's to you."

He passed her the fresh bubbly, and they clinked glasses, leaving Peter to wave his whiskey sour in the air.

"Thank you, Alex. Very kind of you to say so. I wasn't sure that I would hit the right tone, you know?"

"Sure do. I doubt if there was a single person in that audience who was not captivated by your singing."

Marilyn's cheeks reddened slightly, and she took a second sip of her drink. Peter smiled at his companion, and Alex looked around the room.

"Peter, do you mind if I take Marilyn away from you?"

He shrugged and kissed her on the cheek before making his way over to a bar.

"And how do you think I feel about it, Alex?"

"Marilyn, sometimes you just have to trust me and this is one of those occasions."

She smiled back at him and he took her by the hand and led her across to the other side of the room by the incredible book collection. Having reached the edge, they worked their way into the far corner where Bobby was holding sway. As soon as they arrived in the circle of conversation, it fell silent and Alex knew it wasn't because he'd appeared.

Marilyn accepted their congratulations and kisses and ignored the inappropriate fumbling of her ass along the way. Once the wave of admiration abated, Alex took Bobby to one side.

"Marilyn, let me introduce you to Jack's brother, Bobby."

"Very pleased to meet you, Miss Monroe."

"Call me Marilyn. All my friends do."

"Marilyn, you sang like an angel, my dear."

"Thank you. I thought I'd do my best for Jack."

Bobby's eyebrows rose and a crude smile ripped across his face.

"I'm sure you are a constant source of pleasure for my brother."

"We have our moments, Bobby."

Alex detected a hesitation in her speech as if she hadn't quite understood what the attorney general had said, although the lascivious grin was clear to Alex.

"Your singing voice is remarkable. Perhaps later on you might like to give me some lessons?"

"I didn't realize you sang, Bobby?"

"Back in the day, I was a leading light in my fraternity choir, Alex."

"Is that what you called it?"

A glint in Marilyn's eye showed she was getting the joke from earlier and had delivered her own punchline now.

ALEX AND SARAH stayed in town to continue their shopping trip. The following morning, they bumped into Marilyn as she left the Carlyle Hotel via a side entrance and got ready to step into a yellow cab hailed by a bellboy.

"How are you doing?"

"Huh? Oh, good to see you again, Alex."

Marilyn looked askance at Sarah until Alex introduced them. Polite conversation ensued for half a minute, and then Marilyn's eyes darted twice at the open taxi door. Once the vehicle sped away, Sarah commented: "This is an unusual entrance for Monroe to use."

"One of the apartments is owned by Jack, so I'm not surprised Marilyn is departing out of a side door."

Sarah nodded.

"I don't know how Jackie puts up with him."

"Sarah, you assume that she knows what Jack is up to."

She was silent for a spell.

"The wife realizes, Alex. The question is whether she does anything about it."

Now it was Alex's turn to not speak as he mulled over Sarah's comment.

"Was that true for you too, back in the day?"

"I surprised myself when I didn't confront you more, but I believed I would push you further away if I accused you of sleeping with that actress."

"Sarah, I ripped our family apart, not you. And for that, I am forever sorry."

"I forgave you a long time ago, otherwise we wouldn't be here now. We live together, we love together, but we die alone."

BACK HOME, THE reels of Alex's tape recorder rotated while he listened, not moving, not smoking, just caught in the private moments between two people. Most of the session consisted of general noises, but every so often, he heard snatches of conversation as the man and woman spoke between more intimate acts.

"You are so much more of a man than your brother."

"Don't compare him to me. I just want to enjoy our time together."

Muffled sounds followed for ten minutes, but after a while, they stopped fooling around long enough to talk to each other.

"I never want us to be apart. Would you ever be prepared to leave your wife?"

The man laughed, and Alex imagined the look on the woman's face.

"Not while I am in office. The party would never forgive me."

"But later? Then would you?"

Another chortle. "Perhaps, yes. But that will not happen any time soon. I want you to I understand that, right?"

"I guess."

Then she giggled and his breathing increased in intensity, so Alex zoned out and waited for their carnal pursuits to cease.

"I don't know what I'd do if you ever left me."

Marilyn's hushed tone revealed her insecurity as Bobby reassured her that everything would work out just fine.

"Come over here and grab that champagne on your way over."

AUGUST 1962

18

"BOBBY DODGED A bullet, wouldn't you say?"

"How d'you make that out, Sam?"

Alex had paid a visit to Giancana in Miami and they sat at the back of yet another Italian restaurant; never the same place twice.

"With Monroe's overdose, there can be no scandal for the attorney general at any point thanks to his roving dick."

"There is that. She was a beautiful girl."

"I never met her, Alex."

"Marilyn could be really funny if she chose to be, but was sad inside. From what I saw of her, she spent her time fighting with Jayne Mansfield over the affections of our president."

"I thought she kept Bobby's bed warm just before the end."

"That's right, Sam. I reckon she only jumped ship because of the way Jack treated her though. She was loyal."

"Like I said, I only saw her in the movies. Besides, an overdose is not a pretty way to leave this world."

"Marilyn was careful with her meds and her narcotics, and I should know because I supplied her."

"What are you saying, Alex?"

"Nothing at the minute. I'm pointing out that I'd be surprised if Marilyn overdosed by accident. And she didn't come across as a suicidal type."

Sam nodded and continued eating his spaghetti with clams.

ALEX RETURNED HOME to Boyle Heights and amassed all the recordings that had been made in Marilyn's haunts. He listened as her relationship with Bobby deepened. At least from her viewpoint.

"I sure love the time we spend with each other, Bobby."

"Me too, babe."

"Do you ever think we could be together? I mean, for always."

"Not right now, but you never know what might happen in the future."

"You're thinking about your political career, aren't you?"

"And my wife and kids."

"I'd love to have children someday, Bobby."

He instigated none of those conversations, not once in all the hours of talking and banging. Then in July, every tape was filled with the phone ringing and Bobby never picked up. There were times when Marilyn spoke to the emptiness at the other end of the line and that made Alex choke up.

"MASSIMO, I HAVE a discreet job for you, if you're free."

"I am always available to you, Alex."

"The attorney general and Monroe. I'd like you to see what you can find out about their last times together. I'm not interested in what they did between the sheets. I need to learn what they got up to apart from that."

"Do you think that anyone will have seen them? Would they not have been careful about being spotted in public?"

"Massimo, that's for you to find out for me. You are probably right, but I want to know what you can discover."

A couple of weeks later, Massimo visited Alex at home in what he still called the new office. Sarah welcomed him inside and left the two men to their conversation. She knew when Alex wanted to separate her from some of his less savory business activities.

"What have you found out, Massimo?"

"Less than you might hope, Alex."

"Spill."

"Either they were hiding in plain sight or Kennedy and Monroe didn't spend a single moment together in the last three weeks of her life."

"Were they ever in the same city?"

"Yes. Kennedy visited LA at least twice and from all my digging, he might have spent time in a dame's bed, but it sure as hell wasn't with Marilyn Monroe."

Alex ground his molars. He did not know why Bobby's infidelity to Marilyn annoyed him so much, but it did. All he was left with was the recording of her final night when she called Bobby on the phone, but he never picked up. A quick check of hotel records showed he had been in, but the man would not take her call. Only tears, a muffled cry, and then Marilyn was dead.

"I can keep searching if you want me to, Alex, but I've got to tell you I don't think there's anything to find."

"You have done your best, and I thank you. One more thing, you've been looking at this for a while now. Do you believe Bobby had Marilyn killed or was it a suicide?"

Massimo exhaled until there was no air left in his lungs. Then he grabbed a cigarette before replying.

"I've turned up nothing to link him to anywhere she was on the day of her death. If he hired someone to take care of her, then that is something else."

"Massimo, the meds they found by her bed weren't her usual prescription and I'd have known if she had acquired anything else because she'd have bought it from me."

"Blame Kennedy then, but there's nothing we can stick on that man."

November 1963

19

"IT'S BEEN A long time since I have seen you in these parts, Alex."

"I've stayed at home over the last year, Sam, but it sure is good to see you again."

Alex and Giancana sipped cocktails before their pasta arrived. The private dining room at the rear of Sam's restaurant enabled them to speak without any concern over stray ears listening in to their conversation.

"I find it hard to believe you've just sat on your haunches and achieved nothing."

"Sam, at my time of life, I am content to let the money flow in and enjoy the days I spend with my wife. Now and again, we fly over to New York and visit family. But this is the most I've done. Of course, Las Vegas has held my attention."

Sam smiled and waited for the waiter to leave the room, having delivered their plates of spaghetti; clams for him, and salmon for Alex.

"You are too modest, my friend. The gaming capital of the world does not run itself."

"Very kind, Sam. Let's just say I've worked hard to keep a low profile."

"And you have been very successful. I thought the way you handled yourself with the Kennedys was exceptional, Alex."

"No need to blow smoke, Sam. It has been so long since we've broken bread, I guess this isn't just a social call you've asked me to make."

The corners of the Italian's mouth curled upward.

"Let us enjoy our conversation and not worry about any business, for now at least."

A WAITER APPEARED to clear the table of debris and the two fellas placed an order for some coffee. Alex thanked Sam for the offer of a Scotch but declined as he still didn't believe he was in the back of the restaurant just to talk over old times. The drinks were delivered, and the men sat there alone. Alex stirred his coffee to kill time.

"Alex, some of my friends regret what happened in Cuba, but we appreciate your effort despite what transpired in the Bay of Pigs."

"We all lament the outcome with Castro. Some of us had plenty more to lose than others, Sam."

"True, but my younger associates don't have a sense of history. They see what is in front of their noses and remember nothing more than the last smell they inhaled."

"Sam, young men have a lot to learn and I am just glad that I won't have to go back to that country ever again."

Eyes downcast, Sam spoke in a hushed tone.

"There is still much for us to do together, Alex."

"Sam, whatever your next plan to free Havana from the communist hordes, I must count myself out. That is no longer my fight. I got what money I could out of the place and now it is in my past."

"Some of my colleagues fail to recognize the tremendous contribution you continue to deliver to our organization. But I don't make that mistake. Our Vegas interests would be diminished if there wasn't the oversight that you offer us in that open city."

Alex nodded, but Sam still did not meet his gaze.

"Sam, I am sure you remind your less experienced compadres of the value an old Jew can deliver to their wallets."

"You do yourself a disservice, Alex. My father is old, but not you."

"Either way, it won't be too long before I set my affairs in order and retire from this business."

"I am surprised to hear you say that. I thought you'd carry on for years to come."

"Cuba beat Meyer Lansky and I am not that far behind him."

"In that case Alex, I have a proposal for you which should help you feather your nest and hasten your retirement day."

Sam raised his eyes and looked straight at Alex.

"I'd like you to take a trip for me. There may be nothing for you to do when you get there, but I need somebody I trust who knows how to handle himself under any circumstances in case there is trouble."

"Where do you want me to go?"

"Dallas."

"Texas?"

"That's right."

"There's no business there that I can help with, Sam."

"You'd be amazed at what goes on down south. Besides, I'll pay you one hundred thousand if nothing happens and much more depending what else I ask of you while you are in town."

"The last time I did you a favor, I was lucky to get out alive, as were my men. The fact you started this conversation by pointing out that some of your business partners preferred you didn't talk to me makes me want to say no to your request. And I say that with all due respect, Sam."

"You refused a favor from me once before, Alex. Do you remember? And I warned you not to do it again."

"Sam, I was sat between a rock and a hard place in Havana with too many competing interests to keep placated."

"I understand, but it was still a refusal. If I return to my associates and tell them that this Jew shall not help an Italian, how do you think they will respond? These youngsters who can't see further than their noses."

Alex shifted in his seat and took a sip of coffee to moisten the back of his throat.

"Is that how you view me, Sam? As a Jew to do your bidding?"

"Not at all, Alex. But neither of us is so naïve as to believe that other bosses don't hold that view. We have spent too many years fighting common enemies for me to think of you that way."

Sam lit a cigar while Alex pondered.

"I won't be so foolish as to ask you about your business, Sam. But the fact you are asking someone outside your direct sphere of influence within the commission shows it is mighty serious and has a significant amount of danger."

"Life is a risk, Alex."

"What are the chances that Sarah will end up a widow?"

"None that I can see, Alex."

Alex laughed.

"I am sure that's what you told me before I sailed off to the Bay of Pigs."

Sam smiled in return.

"Perhaps, but this time we are not relying on the US Air Force for your safety."

"Should I bring a sniper rifle, Sam?"

"Why no, I am not asking you to shoot anyone, Alex. I want you in the city so that there is a safe distance between any action that needs to be taken and the commission members. You'd be mopping up any potential spilled beer and nothing more."

"More expensive liquor than that we sold during Prohibition if the starting price is one hundred grand."

"Alex, I wish to ensure you are more than taken care of. If I need you, then you must wade in at a moment's notice and if you are not, then the money buys your silence for the rest of your life."

"So, I am a safe pair of hands who isn't tied to the Italian mob?"

"That's the situation in a nutshell."

"Let me sleep on it and tell you tomorrow. Is there somewhere discreet I can stay overnight?"

"WHAT WOULD YOU say if I spent a couple more days where I am and then flew off for a business trip?"

Alex was ensconced in his motel room on the edge of Miami, far from prying eyes. Even so, he chose circumspect language while he spoke with Sarah.

"Did you enjoy your dinner, Alex?"

"The food was good, and the conversation was interesting."

"Why don't you visit Meyer while you are away?"

"I might well do that, but you haven't answered my question."

"Do you think I'm going to? You are your own man, Alex, and you do not need my permission to go on a business trip."

"I'll miss you, Sarah."

"Why are you so sentimental all of a sudden? Is there more to this journey than meets the eye?"

"Indeed. I am not sure what is expected of me and when you consider who invited me over to Miami, you can understand my concerns."

Sarah was silent on the line for a handful of seconds.

"Now you've got me all nervous, Alex."

"That was not the purpose of my call, but I need to think things through with somebody I trust, who is looking after my interests."

"Well, you sure have my attention, Alex."

"Sorry. The other issue is that despite how I feel about this jaunt, I am not sure I can refuse the request anyway."

"If you have no choice, Alex, then you must do what you need to do and there is nothing to debate. Call me when you know you are safe again."

"I'll ring when I arrive back at Boyle Heights."

"At least tell me when you're in California. I love you."

Alex put the phone down and lay on his bed. He took a whiskey from the minibar to help him get to sleep. The next day, he informed Sam he would take the flight to Dallas that night.

"An associate will drive you to the airport at six. Make sure you are ready by then."

20

"GOOD TO SEE you, Meyer."

His old friend nodded but carried on staring at the baseball on the television. One leg hung over the armrest. Lansky remained silent and tutted when a player was out. Alex had never followed the sport and didn't see any reason why he should start now.

"If you're not careful, then I'll have to go before you've said a word to me."

Meyer smiled and pressed a button on the remote control. A single white dot lingered in the middle of the black screen until it vanished.

"My apologies, Alex. The older I get, the more interested I am in watching grown men hit a ball with a stick."

Alex grinned because they both knew that Lansky would have placed several bets on the afternoon's play around the country. He wasn't as retired as he liked everyone to believe.

"Meyer, it's healthy for a fella to enjoy sports, especially if he has some skin in the game."

"I'm not the Big Bankroll fixing the World Series, Alex."

"No you are not, but then Arnold Rothstein didn't put the fix on that result either, as we both know."

They chuckled to themselves and withdrew into their memories of the man who created the five New York families and, along with Charlie Lucky, formed the syndicate to keep the peace between organized crime factions across the country. The mob's commission was an Italian-only version of Rothstein's vision.

"We live in the shadow of greatness, Alex."

"That we do, my friend."

"And I suppose you were just passing and thought you'd drop by for some conversation and cheesecake?"

"If you've got a slice, then I wouldn't say no, Meyer."

Lansky smiled and shuffled out of the room, only to return a moment later with nothing. Then, after five minutes, Thelma appeared holding a tray with a pot of coffee and two pieces of cake.

"Thank you. Are they from a local bakery?"

"Oh no, I import them from New York."

"You can take the fella out of the Five Boroughs…"

Thelma grinned. "It pays to have a few connections from the glory days."

"And I thought you lost everything in Havana, Meyer."

"That was a tragedy, for sure, Alex. But I always maintained several business interests. I never trusted President Batista."

"You behaved like you did, Meyer."

"Only enough to keep him onside, and to ensure that the wheels kept turning on the bus."

"Well, that's all behind us now."

"Alex, we live together, we love together, but we die alone. How can I help?"

Alex waited until Thelma was out of earshot.

"Sam has asked me to do him a favor."

"Giancana?"

"Yes. And I wanted to know your thoughts on the matter."

"Alex, what is it he wants you to do?"

"He hasn't been too up front with the details. I'm to go to Dallas this evening and await further instructions."

"Then why are you asking me? No disrespect, but you've carried out enough contracts not to be concerned about another notch on your rifle?"

"Meyer, that is the strange thing. Sam assures me it's not a hit. I'll be there in case someone else needs assistance."

Lansky cut into his slice and swallowed his first mouthful. Alex did the same and reminded himself how much he enjoyed Lindy's cheesecake.

"So, Alex, either you are a wingman or the fall guy. Which do you think fits the bill?"

"Meyer, if I knew that, we wouldn't be having this conversation."

"You sure are in a pickle."

Alex stared at Lansky and tried to decide if his friend was roasting him or was not engaged with the problem at hand. He must remember to ask Thelma how Meyer was getting on.

"What do you suggest I do? Should I go to Dallas?"

"Is Sam going to pay your expenses?"

"Yes, Meyer."

"Then you have nothing to lose apart from the time you spend there."

"Meyer, this isn't a high school picnic that Sam is organizing."

"Of course not, but whatever it is, he isn't placing you at the center of the action, so you know you will be safe."

"Is it that simple, Meyer?"

"I have no clue at all. I'm bored with this room. Shall we go for a walk?"

ALEX FOLLOWED MEYER out to the patio and his friend sat down again.

"I thought you meant we'd hike around the block, Meyer."

"Now why would I want to wear out a sidewalk when there's this view to admire?"

Alex cast an eye over the deck and pool and the walls surrounding Meyer's property. It was something to look at, but not what you'd call a panorama. Meyer swept his hands under the poolside table.

"No bugs, we can talk here knowing that the Feds won't hear a word we utter."

"Are they monitoring you, Meyer? What for?"

"I have no idea, but it is better to be safe than sorry."

Meyer had never been the paranoid type, but he was making up for it now. So much so that Alex started checking over his shoulder and felt beneath his seat in case the FBI had planted something under his chair. Nothing.

"Meyer, what do you think then?"

"You know how I feel about the Italians, and my position hasn't changed in the last few years."

"Sam has been straight up with me."

"Alex, have you forgotten what happened in the Bay of Pigs?"

"Sam put me in that situation, but it was the US army that failed to keep its word. We were supposed to get air cover for the whole of the first night of the invasion and they delivered bupkis."

"Alex, you are naïve to let the government take the blame. It was Giancana's plan and his failure."

"Meyer, I think the issue is that you've never forgiven Sam for the position he put you in when you were playing both sides in Havana."

"Those Italians have never liked us Jews, and you have always known that. They broke away from the syndicate as soon as they could and formed their own commission."

"Are you going to bring up the Appalachian meeting again? Because that ship set sail five long years ago."

"That was the end, not the beginning. Those Italians thought they were better than us then and they still do now."

Alex didn't respond and counted to five instead.

"You know the irony, Alex?"

"What's that?"

"Sam and his kind propped up Kennedy and brought him into office, and that man has a real soft spot for Jews."

"I've met him, Meyer, and I wouldn't say he has a natural love of the chosen people."

"I've not had the pleasure, but his approach to Israel has been nothing but good. He supports our Jewish homeland and I can't remember a president who's felt that way before."

"Meyer, do you think Jack is pro-Israel because of his liking for Jews, or is it that that lump of desert is just another card for him to play against the Soviets?"

"Alex, you read too many newspapers for your own good. Jack's fighting the communists on all fronts, but he still has time for the Jews. Make no mistake, that is no accident."

"The Kennedys look wonderful on camera but when you see them in the flesh, they are all too human."

"What do I know, Alex, right? All I'm saying is that you shouldn't trust Sam Giancana, but I can't see what can go wrong for you with the Dallas trip if you aren't the trigger man."

21

A MAN ARRIVED at Alex's hotel soon after six and drove him to a private airfield. There was a solitary plane on the runway and the limo stopped one hundred feet from the airstairs. The fella scooted round to Alex's side of the vehicle, opened the door, and escorted him onto the airplane. Not a single word left his mouth for the entire journey.

Inside the jet, a hostess greeted Alex, invited him to sit down, and offered him a drink, which he gladly accepted: Scotch on the rocks. There were five other seats on the plane with a large table positioned next to pairs of seating. Once Alex's glass was resting on his table, the stewardess closed the door and vanished into the cockpit. Alex spotted two men in there, but could only see the backs of their heads.

When they were in the air, the woman returned to give Alex a sealed envelope.

"Have you looked inside this?"

"No, sir. Our instructions were explicit on that matter."

He waited for the woman to sashay to her seat near the cockpit, and then he tore open the envelope to see what Sam had to say for himself. He had the name of a guy he was to mind and the address of an apartment. All he had to do was to reach out and keep in touch with the fella. If there was anything more to the job, then a message would be left at the apartment.

He ripped a hole in the note and placed the piece with the residential address in his pocket. Then he asked for an ashtray. Alex lit a cigarette and then ignited the paper using his lighter until it was nothing more than ash.

A little under three hours later and the jet touched down on a runway in a private airfield.

"Are we in Dallas?"

"On the outskirts, yes, sir. You have a car waiting by the hangar with keys in the ignition. Is there anything else I can get for you?"

ALEX SAT IN his saloon and turned the engine over. On the passenger seat was a map of the city, and he took a few minutes to plan a route to his hideaway. Then he hit the gas, raced out of the airfield, and aimed for downtown Dallas.

He parked on Elm and walked five hundred feet toward North Griffin before finding the apartment block. Deadbeats filled the sidewalks, which reminded Alex of the Bowery before the war.

Inside, he was glad the front door was locked so that he didn't have to climb through more of the winos and punks who littered the frontage. Up to the third floor and the key unlocked the apartment on the first time of asking. It wasn't much to see, but the bedroom appeared clean and the kitchen was well-stocked. If he was only going to be in town for a day or two, then he wouldn't need to show his face in the local store to buy provisions.

Alex put on a pot of coffee and hung his few clothes in the wardrobe by his bed. A shower to wash the cobwebs out of his mind, and he was ready for whatever was to happen next.

BY ELEVEN AT night, Alex didn't think he could bear staring at the blank walls of the living room anymore. Although he knew Sam would not want him to be seen around town, he took his chances and hit the street. With his coat collar turned up to hide his face, Alex strode along the sidewalk. The drunks congregated four doors down from his apartment block in front of a general store, panhandling for enough money to buy some booze, but Alex was in no mood to deal with them.

Around the corner, the block emptied, and he felt as though this was a different city. Outside each of the buildings stood a concierge waiting for the residents to return and at the far end of the street, Alex noticed a cop walking the beat.

There was no need to head straight into potential danger, so he sauntered along the sidewalk about half a block until he reached Fred's Bar. He entered and aimed for his usual preference, a booth at the back of a drinking establishment, a location often reserved for doting couples and therefore not well lit.

A waitress delivered a Scotch within a minute of Alex placing his order. Efficient service, he thought. Five minutes later and Alex saw the cop meander past the front of the bar.

The place was only half full, the majority couples, but there was one table of four young men who were already rowdy enough to earn annoyed expressions from some of the nearby patrons. Alex took measured sips of his drink and let the world flow by.

Two jugs of ale later and their waitress had had enough. One guy slapped her on the ass as she walked away from the table. She turned back and poured a glass of beer over the offender's head. The guy leaped to his feet, and the bartender ran out from behind the bar. If there had been a piano, then the player would have stopped by now. Alex stayed where he was.

The boy formed a fist and pulled his arm back as if to take a swipe at the barman, who remained still. Meanwhile, the waitress edged out of harm's way and stood next to the bar. They all hovered in this Mexican stand-off for two, maybe three, seconds, and then one of the boy's friends placed a hand on his shoulder and whispered something in his ear. The guy lowered his fist, and the four left without another word or a punch thrown.

Alex finished his drink as slowly as his first few sips. Just as he'd allowed the last drop to flow down the back of his throat, the waitress appeared to ask if he wanted another.

"Don't mind if I do. You handled yourself well earlier on, by the way."

"Thanks. They're good kids most of the time but can get fresh once they've had too many beers inside them."

"So they are regulars, then? Fred knew how to handle himself."

"Who? Fred?" She laughed. "Hank sorted those boys out. Fred's just a name on the sign outside."

"My mistake. No offense to Hank."

"None taken, Mac."

A moment later and Alex's Scotch arrived.

"You're not from around here, are you, Mac?"

"Just passing through."

"Well, I hope you have time to see a few tourist attractions before you leave. There's a parade tomorrow…"

"I'm in town on business, so there won't be much of an opportunity for sightseeing. Thank you, anyway."

The waitress shrugged and walked away, leaving Alex to drink his Scotch in peace.

22

AN HOUR AFTER speaking to Sarah on a payphone the following morning, and Alex had had enough of aimless walking and returned to his apartment. He sat down for two minutes but knew that he needed to walk again. With no other place to go, he headed to Fred's and occupied the same booth as he'd been in the previous night.

Within thirty seconds of sitting down, Amy appeared.

"Hi, I'll start with a coffee. Do you have any cake I could try?"

"Good to see you back. We have a vanilla cheesecake or…"

"That sounds perfect."

She smiled and sashayed away to fulfill his order. The coffee and cake arrived less than a minute later. Alex drew a sip of the brew and almost immediately regretted it: the pot had been on the burner for too long. Fred's didn't have sufficient morning customers to get the filter jug refreshed often enough.

He then took a bite out of the cheesecake and dropped his fork on the plate. This wasn't baked cheesecake. Alex washed away the taste of the cake with the acrid flavor of the burned coffee. This was not turning out to be a good day.

At this point, Hank switched on the television and changed channel to the local news. Somewhere in the city, people were lining the sidewalks. The angle of the screen from Alex's viewpoint was too narrow for him to make out any image that well, but he had a general idea about what was going on. Amy returned.

"How's the cake, dear?"

"Can I be honest with you?"

"For sure."

"It doesn't taste like baked cheesecake and the coffee is burned."

Amy's smile fell from her face. She blinked once.

"I'm so very sorry. Let me get you a fresh brew right away and let me offer you a slice of coffee cake instead?"

"Thank you. A new mug would be great. I didn't ask you what kind of cheesecake you had, so that's not your fault."

"I told you last night, you weren't from round here. That is the only cheesecake Texans know."

"It's not a big deal, but yes, I'll try the coffee cake, but you must charge me for both portions, understand?"

Amy removed everything she'd placed on his table and flew off to the kitchen. Alex heard raised voices over the volume of the television broadcast and she appeared with a large slice of cake.

"This is on the house and I'll have no more talk on the matter."

Then she scurried away and Alex waited five minutes for a fresh pot of coffee to brew and a piping hot mug to be delivered to his table.

"I hope this is better for you."

"I'm sure it is, Amy."

She looked down at her name badge, pinned over her heart, and smiled again.

"You're welcome…"

"Call me David."

Alex beamed back at Amy.

"Let me know if you need anything else."

Alex nodded, and she walked away to the bar, and to monitor the java more closely than she had before.

The cake was a little dry but edible, and the coffee was adequate. This was a local bar: Alex expected nothing more from it.

The barman cranked up the volume of the television and Alex heard a commentator talking about the parade Amy had mentioned the night before. Sounded like it wasn't that far from where he was sitting. He watched as a steady stream of people hastened from right to left, many holding miniature Stars and Stripes on little sticks.

Alex concentrated on his food and drink and tried his best to ignore the rest of the world. His sole purpose in being in this city was a man about whom he had yet to receive any instructions to go anywhere near. He just needed to sit the day out and wait in case something happened.

The commentator on the television let out a piercing scream and everyone else in Fred's stood up. Women shrieked, and the barman put the volume on maximum, but Alex had no idea what was going on. He looked around for Amy, but she was nowhere to be seen.

A man took his wife in his arms as she blubbed away and others slammed their fists on their tables. The ones nearest the front ran outside and headed left—in the direction of the parade. Not wanting to appear different from the rest, Alex stood and leaned forward as his waitress hustled past, a tear in her eye.

"What's happened, Amy?"

"Couldn't you see? The president's been shot."

Alex felt a dull ache in the pit of his stomach and he knew he had to get the hell out of the joint.

ALEX CHUCKED SOME greenbacks on the table and ran out of the bar. He too turned left, but he was not planning on going anywhere near the scene of the hit. Instead, he hightailed it to his apartment and slammed the door shut behind him. He threw himself into an armchair and tried to get his bearings. Sam had taken a contract out on Jack. Alex swallowed hard to find some saliva at the back of his throat and coughed instead.

He switched on the radio to see if he could find out more about what had happened to Jack. The commentator spoke of several shots fired, and that Kennedy had been hit and was on his way to Parkland Memorial Hospital. There was no word on whether anybody else had been injured. Alex rocked in his armchair. Sam had taken out a contract on the president!

Another guy in the car, Governor Connally, had been shot too but was alive. Jackie had survived without a mark on her. Just as the voice from the radio confirmed that Kennedy had been pronounced dead, the phone rang.

"Don't do anything. You might still be needed. Stay where you are for the next twenty-four hours."

"Understood." Then a click, and the phone went dead.

Alex popped his head out of the living room window and saw that all the cars had stopped in their tracks. Drivers stood with their doors open and radios on. A silence had descended on the city as people soaked in the implications of the Dealey Plaza assassination. Soon after, Lyndon Johnson was sworn in as the new president.

As he listened some more, Alex heard birds chirping outside, and he closed the sash window tight shut. Entering the bedroom for no good reason, something made him lift the mattress, always a convenient hiding place back in the day when he ran Murder Corporation and needed a safe location to stash items.

Sure enough, there was a pistol and two boxes of slugs. The butt had tape wrapped around it the same as the trigger. This was to be used for a job where the owner did not want their fingerprints to turn up. Was this gun for him or had it been hidden by some unknown assailant on a previous hit? Alex left it where he'd found it for now, and made the bed again.

He tried sitting in the living room, but within a minute, he was pacing up and down. This was no good, not at all. Alex had lost count of how many men he had killed. Yes, he had attempted to hit Castro and had even whacked his friend Benny Siegel, but an American president? There was no way he wanted to be caught up with anything like that. Sam should have told him, explained the situation, allowed him to make his own choices. Meyer was right, you can't trust the Italians.

Alex grabbed his keys and left the apartment, ignoring what the disembodied voice at the end of the phone had instructed. He couldn't be cooped up in that place a second longer. As he bundled along the sidewalk, Alex failed to notice how empty the neighborhood was. Even the drunks were showing their respect for the fallen Kennedy. He turned the corner and strode toward Fred's Bar.

Inside, Amy was sweeping the floor, and the joint seemed deserted. He pushed the door, but it was locked shut. She looked up from her work and held one finger up, indicating for Alex to wait. She put her mop in its bucket and opened up.

"Are you still serving? I've nowhere else to go."

"Hank doesn't want us to draw a crowd, but as you were in earlier on, I don't see why not."

She twisted her head to look at Hank, who nodded his consent. Alex went back to his booth and ordered a Scotch.

"To Jack," he muttered under his breath and knocked the drink down in one. He sipped his second glass and, having calmed down, he slunk out of the bar and returned to the apartment to await further instructions.

23

THE PHONE RANG soon after Alex finished in the shower the next morning.

"Contact our mutual friend. Monitor him and nothing more, for now."

Before he could ask anything, his instructor had ended the call. The mark owed Sam big time, the result of gambling debts that had mounted up over a matter of months. Small amounts that got out of hand on account of the fella doubling up once too often and the size of the vig Sam's associates charged.

The first port of call was to the Carousel Club, three blocks east and one south of Fred's, which was a simple walk from the apartment. There were a few people on the streets, but it was still quite early. On the same block, there were other clubs and bars and a general store interspersed between the residences.

It might have been eight in the morning, but the place was shut tight. A piece of paper was pinned to the door, announcing that the joint would remain closed for the next few days out of respect for Kennedy's death. Alex tried to peer through the windows, but there was nothing to see. The darkened glass prevented anybody from getting a free view of the interior. If his mark was inside, he wasn't making any noise.

Rather than wait around hoping to find someone entering a closed joint, he hopped a cab over to Oak Lawn and wandered the streets until he reached the Vegas Club.

It was in as salubrious an area as the Carousel; the trendy in Dallas were not Ruby's target market. Judging by their surroundings, Alex guessed the joints would take money from anyone who wanted a drink. They were far removed from Alex's blind pigs when he'd sold liquor during Prohibition. Back then, he'd boasted the rich and the famous as his patrons. Looking at the exterior of the Vegas, Alex wondered what kind of fella he was going to tangle with.

This club was closed too and a similar note was placed on its entrance. He was standing there trying to figure out his next move when a woman appeared and headed for the door. She looked up and stopped in her tracks.

"Were you expecting the club to be open too?" he asked.

"Yes, bud. And you are…?"

"A friend. I owe Ruby money and wanted to pay him back."

A smile. "You owe him green? I don't think I've ever heard that happen since I started working here."

"It's only a hundred bucks, but I sure would like to give it to him. I wouldn't want to get into any trouble."

"He can wig out at a moment's notice."

"Do you reckon he'll open up later on?"

"You can read, bud?" She flicked a finger at the announcement pinned to the door.

"But you thought the club would be open today, otherwise what are you doing here?"

"True. We closed around two this morning and Jack said he wanted us back, but he must have changed his mind."

"At a moment's notice?"

She laughed and nodded.

"Patty Ingham, by the way."

"Call me David."

"Ruby owes me back pay. So if you give him his cash, then I might see some money myself."

Patty gave Alex the same address that was in Sam's note, wished him well, and strolled off down the street. After she vanished around the corner, he went in the opposite direction for a couple of blocks and waited a lifetime to hail a cab.

WHEN ALEX GOT out of the taxi, he recognized where he had been dropped, a short hop from Fred's and one block from the Carousel. He had already strode down this sidewalk earlier in the day. Alex glanced up and down the street until he was certain he wasn't about to bump into his mark. Then he checked again to see if he saw anyone he knew. The last thing he needed was for a local like Amy to spot him and place him in the vicinity.

Still only a handful of people were on the streets and most folk were at home with their televisions on, watching to find out about Lee Harvey Oswald, who had been arrested the same day as Jack was killed and remained in police custody. Alex was not as concerned about Oswald's fate as he was to discover what he would do with Ruby once he caught up with him. Across the street, two doors down, was an alleyway. Alex would have preferred to watch from a cafe so he could at least have a coffee and a bite to eat, but everywhere was shut. The president had been dead less than twenty-four hours and the country had descended into a state of mourning.

He leaned on a wall in the shadows of the alleyway entrance and hoped Ruby would arrive sooner rather than later. One hour on, and Alex's hopes had faded as he finished the last cigarette in his pack. He rotated his lighter in his pocket just for something to do. His patience was wearing thin, in part in reflection of him not knowing what Sam had in store for Ruby at Alex's hands.

Alex told himself to give Ruby another thirty minutes because there was no guarantee the fella would even show. He might be holed up with a skirt somewhere and as much as Alex wanted to earn his fee, there was no way in hell he was going to stand in this alleyway for an entire day and night.

When the designated amount of time had elapsed, Alex stood straight and peered up and down the road. There was only a couple in the distance, sauntering away from him. No sign of Ruby or anybody else in his vicinity. With a heavy sigh, Alex took two steps forward and onto the sidewalk. A glance left and right, and still no one showed. He turned left, strolled to the end of the block, stopped, then looked behind. A man turned up the opposite side of the street, heading toward Ruby's building or the alleyway. Alex fumbled with a loose shoelace so that he could steal a few seconds to figure out if this guy was a person of interest.

As Alex had hoped, the fella stopped in front of Ruby's apartment block, took out a key, and let himself in. Alex sighed again as he realized he would need to resume his position in the alleyway. Of course, the fact the guy lived in the same building did not make him Ruby and he had been too far away for Alex to see his features. Not that he had a photo to work off, but Sam's instructions had been careful to let Alex know that the mystery mark was Jewish. And the guy on the other side of the road had a big enough nose to fit the description.

He skirted around the back of the apartment block and saw motion on the third floor. At the front, Alex scanned the names on the mailboxes and, based on their formation, he reckoned Ruby was a third-floor occupant. The odds were stacking up in his favor, but there was only one way to be certain.

Alex rang the bell of apartment 3D and a gruff voice responded through the intercom.

"Yes?"

"Package for Mr. Jack Ruby."

"I'm not expecting anything… Hello? Hello?"

That was all Alex needed to know, so he left the fella hanging and scurried down the street three hundred feet before crossing the road to get a better view of the entrance.

24

AN HOUR LATER, Ruby appeared at the front entrance and hustled down the street, with Alex tailing him half a block behind. He would have got closer, but the streets were too empty and he didn't want to be spotted. Around the corner and into a liquor store.

Alex held back a few seconds and then used the opportunity to get much tighter to the fella. He picked up his pace, walked into the outlet, and headed straight for the counter.

"Bottle of Scotch, please."

Ruby arrived behind him to wait in line. The store owner shook his head.

"I got Irish but not Scotch."

Alex turned round to face Ruby. "What kind of town is this?"

Ruby shrugged. "The city has been good to me."

Alex shot back and accepted the whiskey. Then he paid and pretended to sort out his pockets while Ruby handed over some green to cover the cost of his milk and pack of cigarettes.

"I'm sorry about before. This whole business with Oswald has got me all shaken up."

"Don't give it a moment's thought. It's bad enough that it happened without the damn thing occurring by your back door."

Alex looked puzzled for a minute, then raised his eyebrows.

"Of course, Dealey Plaza isn't that far from here."

Ruby nodded and eyed him up and down.

"Are you visiting these parts?"

"Yes, I'm here on business for a week."

"With anyone?"

"Nope."

"Nobody should be on their own on days like these. Want to share some of that bottle back at mine?"

Alex waited a few seconds, as though he was pondering the situation.

"Sounds as though we've got ourselves a plan. Call me David."

INSTEAD OF TAKING him to his apartment, Ruby led Alex over to the Carousel Club. Once inside, Ruby cleared the bar and arranged a couple of stools.

"This can't be where you live?"

"No, but it is mine."

Alex whistled with approval and appreciation.

"Mighty fine. You've done well for yourself."

"I get by, David. You wanted a Scotch, right?"

A nod and Ruby fixed Alex a shot.

"Ice?"

Alex shook his head and his host placed the glass on the counter and poured himself a vodka tonic.

"Kennedy was a great man, David."

They raised their glasses and Alex knocked back his whisky. Ruby poured him another.

"So, how long have you run this joint?"

"A few years, I guess. Let me show you around."

The main bar stood in front of a dance floor and there was space for a band in the far corner. Through a doorway was a gaming room with two roulette wheels and several card stations. Another impressed whistle from Alex. Then Ruby took him to a third area behind a locked door.

"This is for my VIPs."

Alex surveyed the reception desk and Ruby showed him into each of the private rooms. Most had a massage table and a couch, but there was one with a heart-shaped bed and silk sheets reserved for Ruby's high rollers—men who were prepared to spend more than a Jackson on a girl.

"You sure are doing well for yourself."

Alex offered the lie so Ruby would feel better about himself, but even with this joint, Alex knew he could make it profitable without too much effort. Ruby must be a complete schlemiel in business to be up to his neck in debt to Sam and own at least two bars like this.

"Is this your only place?"

"No, I have another bar and a few other interests."

"I'm surprised you have time to sleep."

"David, there's no need to blow smoke up my ass. You said you're in business too. How do you make your money?"

"I am a troubleshooter, you might say. I help my clients with any problems they may have. And, like you, I have a few interests on the side."

"That sure sounds like an interesting time. Hopping from one place to another. Don't you ever want to settle down and stay in one town to grow roots?"

"I've got that too. I'm based in California and visit my kids on the East Coast several times a year."

"The traveling would destroy me. After the war, I moved here from San Francisco and vowed that was the last time I'd pull up stakes and relocate."

"You get used to the planes and trains. It gives me a chance to relax and take stock."

They wandered back to the bar and Ruby filled their glasses.

"David, I'm keeping my bars closed for another day or two, so there's going to be no action here tonight. Do you fancy sharing a meal at mine? My sister's cooking is to die for and we've always got a spare seat for a stranger in town. Nobody should be alone so soon after Kennedy passed."

EVA GRANT WELCOMED the two men into Ruby's apartment and Alex wondered why she cooked for her brother and whether her husband was still in the picture. Either way, Ruby was right, the food she was cooking smelled great.

"This is David. He's a stranger in town and I've asked him over for dinner."

"Pleased to meet you."

"Charmed, I'm sure. What's in the oven? It smells good enough to eat."

She smiled and mentioned chicken schnitzel.

"Just like my mama used to make, Eva."

Ruby raised an eyebrow.

"Are you a member of the brotherhood?"

"Yes, but not practicing. I hope that doesn't cause you any offense."

"Not at all. My sister and I haven't been to *shul* since we were kids."

"I can't say I've seen the inside of a synagogue any more recently myself."

They all chuckled and Eva announced that their food was ready.

Ruby's apartment wasn't large enough to have a separate dining room, and they ate at the kitchen table. A small yappy mutt sought attention from Ruby from the moment they sat down. After way too much barking for Alex's liking, Ruby relented and threw Sheba a piece of the schnitzel. Eva tutted.

"What was that for? Are you judging how I feed my dog?"

Eva remained silent as Ruby's cheeks reddened.

"I'll do whatever I want with that dachshund."

Ruby cut off another chunk and fed Sheba from his hand.

"Jacko, don't start on me. Not when we have a guest with us."

Ruby looked over at Alex as if for the first time. Alex did his best to placate him with a neutral expression and carried on eating; the schnitzel was a little tough, but he wasn't intending on raising a complaint. The rosemary potatoes were cooked to perfection.

"Do not tut me, Eva. You know I don't like that."

"I'm sorry, Jacko. I didn't mean nothing by it."

There was silence for ten seconds, and then Alex lightened the mood.

"You mentioned you came from San Francisco. Is that where you were born?"

"Chicago."

"Small world. I knew some fellas from there. Between the wars." Ruby's expression relaxed.

"That so? I had business dealings with some connected fellas too, back in the day."

"Like who?"

"David, have you heard of Al Capone?"

"You're kidding me. You met Alfonse?"

"Once or twice. He was a great guy."

"Sure was."

Alex thought back to the time he'd visited the gangster before his death. A shell of the man who once ruled the Windy City and worked with Alex during the Prohibition years.

"Who else did you know back then, David?"

He had said too much already.

"The usual crew. I'm sure you've got some tales to tell."

"While Capone was sitting in his silk drawers raking in the cash, I was on the street, hustling the great people of Chicago with my racing tips."

"Jacko, don't undersell yourself." His sister nudged Ruby in the arm.

"You'll make me blush, Eva. I'd help the neighborhood bagman to carry out his collections."

"Those must have been exciting times."

"They were, but you'd have had your fair share of excitement if you knew Al?"

"That was a long time ago. I paid the price for my youthful choices."

"Amen to that, David. And there's nothing to worry about with us. Eva and I don't hold a fella's past against him. I've been in the same situation."

"To youthful indiscretions!"

They raised their wine glasses to Alex's toast and resumed the meal with no further outbursts from Ruby.

"David, the funny thing is that nowadays, half the Dallas police force are members of one of my clubs. If they only knew what I was like back in the day."

Ruby chuckled, and Alex smiled in return.

"It must be a good feeling to know that your clubs are protected without needing to rely on other insurance options."

"We pay our dues, same as everybody else, David."

"This is a mighty fine schnitzel, Eva. Thank you for tonight's meal. I do appreciate it."

"You are very kind, David. I always cook more than we need, so it was my pleasure. Besides, Sheba doesn't have to eat a human's portion of chicken, does she, Jacko?"

"Don't get me started again."

They all laughed this time, as there was no edge to Ruby's voice.

25

ALEX OFFERED TO help clear the dishes, but Ruby wouldn't let him; that was what his sister was for. Instead, the men walked out to the living room and settled in with a bottle of Scotch for Alex and Ruby's vodka nearby. Once the splashing noises of Eva's washing up had abated, she sat down to join them, but Ruby's expression showed she was not welcome so she made her excuses and went to her bedroom.

"How long have you and Eva been sharing an apartment?"

"Ever since that meeskait of a husband died on her."

"And you've never married?"

"I have Sheba for company and Eva for meals and laundry. What would I do with a wife?"

Alex opened his mouth to answer and then closed it again. Ruby's eyes sparkled.

"So you meet girls in your bars then?"

"A club is like a babe magnet and if I hit a dry patch, then I just advertise for another waitress."

"You sure have all the angles covered."

They drank a toast to Ruby's success and shot the breeze for longer than Alex could believe. That man could not stop talking: about himself and how brilliant he was in the sack, in business, with his family. If half of what he claimed was true, then Ruby should have been a millionaire and not an indebted bum, which is what he was.

"And another thing... I can't believe how good Kennedy has been for Israel, David."

"How so?"

"I reckon he is the first president to support the country against the Arabs surrounding that beautiful place."

"Have you ever been?"

"Not yet, but I hope to someday. The country is steeped in milk and honey."

"That's what the Bible says."

"I might not be a regular in a synagogue, but I still believe in the *Torah*. Don't you, David?"

"The truth is, I'm not sure what I think anymore. When I was a kid, I think I believed in God, but now? What I saw on the fields of France left me doubting."

"I was in this man's army in the Second World War."

"Did you see any action?"

"No, I was a mechanic in a US base."

"Well, at least you did your bit against the Japanese and the Nazis."

"That's what I'm talking about, David. Kennedy was helping us Jews stand up against today's threat from the Arabs."

"Kennedy will have had his reasons for sure. Do you feel threatened by Arabs in Dallas?"

"No, David, but there's anti-Semitism at home too. I was in the local newspaper office yesterday when Oswald did for Kennedy and I saw some evil adverts the paper was accepting. It made my blood boil."

"What were you doing there?"

"I advertise the clubs to increase footfall."

"People have hated the Jews ever since Moses walked the earth."

"But now, David, we've lost a protector in the form of Kennedy. Lee Harvey Oswald is an anti-Semite."

"You don't know that. If he wanted to attack Jews, then there are many more direct ways of going about it than killing Kennedy."

"The consequence of his actions means the Jews will have a harder time, David."

"You may be correct."

"Listen, David. I told you I knew most of the Dallas police force, right?"

"Sure."

"Well, they let me come and go in their buildings, so I thought I'd head to the press conference they held yesterday after the shooting. If you had heard with your own ears what some of those cops told me who were close to the case, then you'd be convinced that Oswald was an anti-Semite."

"Him and the rest of the goyishe world."

"David, I don't know why you are defending this vermin."

"I am not. I have many reasons for wanting Jack Kennedy to be alive, but that does not mean that Oswald killed him because he supported Israel. That's my point, and nothing more."

Ruby glared at him and Alex took a sip from his Scotch to defuse the situation. After a silent spell, Ruby's cheeks seemed less red.

"I apologize if I caused you any offense."

"That's all right, David. You are a guest in my home and I showed you disrespect by raising my voice. I am the one who should say sorry."

"Then let us both accept that there is more that binds us than can split us apart and not allow a minor disagreement to change that. I think I speak for both of us when I say that Lee Harvey Oswald deserves to die."

EVA POPPED HER head around the door.

"Is Jacko causing trouble, David?"

"No, everything is fine, thanks."

"I heard a ruckus and wondered if you boys were behaving yourselves."

"No, dear, we were just talking politics."

"And with a guest in our home. You should know better."

She shook her head and walked out, leaving Ruby to gaze downward as his cheeks reddened.

"Sometimes, she acts more like my mother than a sister."

"Both are precious to us."

"I'll drink to that, David."

After a sip of his Scotch, Alex decided that now was as good as any other time to cut to the chase.

"You might not know this, but we have a mutual acquaintance."

"Who's that, David?"

"The fella who holds your IOUs."

Ruby's arm lowered just as he was about to take a swig of his vodka tonic, suspicion oozing out of every pore.

"What do you mean, David?"

"Let's not pretend. You owe our mutual friend a five-figure sum."

"Who are you talking about?"

"Are you going to force me to mention his name? I thought we were all gentlemen here."

"How do I know you aren't some sort of shakedown artist?"

Alex sighed.

"Because you are still alive. If I wished you any kind of harm, then I would have done something before now. Either when we were alone in the Carousel Club or when you first brought me home to meet your sister. I intend neither of you any ill will, but you and I have some business to conduct."

Alex allowed his remarks to sink in with Ruby, who was confused and unsure what to say next. His jaw opened and closed twice with no words leaving his lips. After half a minute, a thought departed his mouth.

"Giancana sent you."

Alex nodded and lit a cigarette. He flicked some tobacco off his knee.

"That wasn't an accidental meeting in the liquor store."

A second nod and Ruby knocked back the rest of his drink. Then he sat forward and poured himself another shot of vodka. Alex popped into the kitchen to find some tonic water. When he returned,

Ruby stood facing the living room door with a pistol in his hand, aimed at Alex's chest.

"Put that away before you hurt somebody."

"I know how to use this thing and don't tell me otherwise."

"Ruby, if you fire that gun at me, you'd better make certain you kill me straight off because if you do not, then I guarantee you won't be alive in the morning. Second, with whatever breath I have left, Eva will get hers. And if those aren't good enough reasons, Sam will send someone else to visit you and he'll torture you before he kills you, slower than you can ever imagine."

Alex stayed still to let Ruby think through his actions.

"Like I said, put the gun down so we may talk business."

Ruby's arm relaxed, and he slumped in his chair. He allowed the pistol to drop to the floor, and Alex grabbed it to examine the firearm.

"Putz, there are no slugs in the chamber. Next time you try to shoot a fella, make sure you know what you are doing."

Alex placed the gun on the table adjacent to his Scotch and lit another cigarette. Under any other circumstances, this guy would have been dead by now, but Alex used all his inner reserves to control his temper. Meyer was right, every time he did Sam a favor, he ended up risking his life. What if Ruby had fired as soon as he got back to the room? Life was way too short for *gonifs* to pull this kind of crap.

"Have you calmed down, Ruby?"

"Yes, but—"

"If you are going to get fresh with me, then you are not ready to discuss business. And I need to know that I have your full attention before we talk."

"It's just—"

"There will be no questions from you. I have a simple proposition that you must hear and agree to. Assuming that you find it acceptable then we can figure out all the details once you have the offer."

"Let me apologize for my actions, David. I got scared and didn't think through what I was doing."

"Are you ready to listen now?"

"Sure thing, David."

"By tomorrow night, you'll have the debt that you owe Sam wiped clean."

"What do I have to do?"

26

IN THE MORNING, Alex walked over to Ruby's apartment and the local drove them both to Main Street and the location of a money transfer service.

"Put the car in the lot over there."

"But it'll cost gelt, David."

"Ruby, now is not the time to count pennies. Let's get this vehicle off the road."

Jacko nodded acceptance and hauled into the parking lot half a block further on. Alex instructed him to go to the far end of the space so that the eyes of the attendant were not on them. Once Ruby had pulled on the handbrake, he whipped out his revolver.

"Take it easy and put that thing below the dashboard. We can't have you being seen brandishing a firearm."

"Sorry, David. I wasn't thinking."

Alex cleared his throat. "You need to get your head in the game, man."

Ruby continued to point the barrel of the gun in Alex's general direction.

"Anyone would think you're planning on shooting me."

A nervous laugh emanated from the owner of the Carousel Club.

"Remember what I said to you last night, Ruby. You can get out from under a pile of debt and your sister will be looked after for the rest of her life. Killing me will bring down a world of pain and agony for you and her. So check your weapon and put it away."

Ruby lowered the revolver and popped it in his pocket.

"Sorry, but I'm nervous."

"That's as may be but we need you to stay focused. It's going to be a long day and we want you to be in one piece by the end, right?"

Ruby nodded, and Alex lit him a cigarette. They hopped out of the car and the club owner handed over his keys to the attendant. Alex made sure he had already hustled past before the guy had left his kiosk. Then they walked onto the road and headed left.

Half a block down and Alex got Ruby to pop into a general store and buy a pack of cigarettes and a newspaper. Then two blocks on and Ruby went into a bank to take out some green. Again, Alex ensured he stayed on the street. The aim was for as many people as possible to see Ruby, to remember his face and the fact that he was alone.

With the cash in his wallet, Ruby returned to Alex's side, and they carried on sauntering along Main Street.

"Is David your real name?"

"What do you think?"

"I doubt if it is, but it is a strong Biblical name."

"Thank you."

"How did you know I was getting cold feet?"

"What do you mean, Ruby?"

"That I was thinking of welshing on my deal with Sam."

"I had no idea. You seem to think I am something more than a go-between."

"David, from what you've said, you come across as well-connected and sound pretty tight with Giancana, so I just assumed."

"For this job, I'm only a hired hand, but it is no accident that we are together right now. If our mutual friend felt you might not go through with the plan, then I was a natural person to turn to."

"Sam and I have had this agreement in place for weeks, if not months."

"So, Ruby, why did you allow me to think I needed to convince you to get involved in this?"

"David, it amused me. You were coming on so thick and strong, I figured I'd let you play out your hand. Besides, what you said reminded me of why I agreed to do this in the first place."

"I'm glad I have been so entertaining for you."

"David, what I maintained about Kennedy and Israel was all true. I believe his death needs to be avenged. We mustn't let the anti-Semites win."

RUBY BOUGHT A slice of pizza and a coffee from a concession and Alex did the same a minute later and caught up with him around the corner.

"Don't you think it's a bit early for lunch?"

Alex looked at his watch and saw that it was just after eleven.

"Maybe, but we've been up for hours and it is always sensible to operate on a full stomach, wouldn't you say?"

Ruby smiled and nodded.

"It sure tastes great, huh, David?"

"There is nothing like the flavors of street food to keep fellas like us on our toes."

They polished off their pizza, and Ruby slugged his coffee down in almost one gulp. Alex preferred frequent sips to avoid burning the roof of his mouth. Brunch over, the men walked from their South Saint Paul rest stop one block east to North Harwood where there was a fund transfer store.

"I'll stay here while you hand that money over."

Ruby nodded. The least the fella could do was to send Patty's back pay over to her. On the other side of the street, from the corner of South Harwood and Main down to Commercial Street, stood the headquarters of the Dallas Police Department. Alex scuttled over the road while avoiding the front entrance.

Fifty feet toward Commercial, Alex found a ramp leading down to the basement. He scampered down the slope to discover a locked glass door. Alex whipped out a small piece of wire from his jacket pocket and positioned it in the crack between the lock and the jamb.

A few seconds later, it was unlocked, and Alex fixed the latch to remain open.

Heading back to the other side of the street he found Ruby waiting, smoking a cigarette. Even from this distance, the two men saw a large huddle in front of the main entrance.

"They must have been damn busy since Dealey Plaza, David."

"And some. Are you ready?"

"Now?"

"They'll be moving Oswald from his cell soon to take him to a holding facility."

"A jail?"

"Yes, until he stands trial. The police headquarters isn't a hotel."

"I suppose not."

Ruby flicked the remnants of his cigarette onto the ground and stepped on its smoldering remains. He put a hand inside his jacket and transferred the gun into his pants pocket. A quick nod and Ruby paced himself as he crossed the street. Alex remained where he was until Ruby vanished down the ramp. Then he wandered over to the main entrance of the police building along South Harwood and joined the crowd.

MOST OF THE people outside police headquarters were doing nothing much at all. They stood and stared at the main entrance, hoping to catch sight of Oswald. On the other side of the crowd, a young man held a radio next to his ear, but he was too far away for Alex to hear anything from it.

A car backfired some way off and the throng surged forward. The kid with the radio ran down the street, followed by at least twenty others. Two cops stormed out of the entrance, brandishing their weapons. The men and women, who had been so eager to enter the building a few seconds before, stopped in their tracks.

"You know what's happening, bud?"

Alex shook his head and noticed that he was in the middle of the crowd. He let others push in front to hear what the cops were saying, and he continued moving away until he was at the back of the huddled mass.

He glanced up and down the street, but the kid and his followers had not returned and were nowhere to be seen. A ripple of applause spread across the group, and Alex was careful to join in, although there was no reason for the appreciation.

A man standing in front of Alex turned to his pal. "They've killed Oswald. That sonofabitch got his."

Alex leaned forward. "You heard who did it?"

"Nope. It happened just a minute ago."

"How d'you know?"

"I was at the front and listened to one of the cops talking."

That was good enough for Alex. Ruby had done what was asked of him, and now it was time to leave. He waited for a count of thirty, put his hands in his pants pockets, and walked up to Main Street. On his way, he passed the ramp, which was now filled with cops and bystanders. Without missing a beat, Alex kept to his plan, turning west, then north until he reached Elm Street.

He ensured he maintained a casual pace to avoid garnering any attention and made one last sweep of the apartment in case he had missed anything in his packing. Baggage in hand, he scurried down the stairs and into his car, then headed north and west until he connected with North Houston and punched the gas to take him away from the center of the city.

Five minutes later, he pulled the vehicle over and lit a cigarette. Then he turned the vehicle around and headed back south—there was unfinished business to take care of.

27

ALEX HAD GOT Patty's home address from Ruby when he was looking up her records to get the wire transfer details. She had seen Alex when he asked about Ruby and that was too close a connection to be left dangling.

He parked three blocks from her apartment and walked from there. To his regret, she lived on the fifth floor. Alex went round the back of the building and started the journey up the fire stairs until he reached her window. Then he stopped to catch his breath; he wasn't getting any younger.

He peered into a kitchen/diner and saw Patty sitting at a table with a mug of coffee. Alex checked out the window frame and pulled a tool from his inside jacket pocket to jimmy the sash open as quietly as possible. Perhaps because she had her back to him, he'd raised the window and swung a foot onto the floor before she turned around and gasped.

"You?"

Her memory for faces vindicated Alex's decision to resolve the matter, and he scrambled in and took one step forward. Patty inhaled to scream, but the rear of Alex's hand slapped her sideways and she bumped her head on the corner of the table as she went down.

He checked her pulse: alive. He raised her shoulders, and she slumped back down. So Alex had some time to think. Ruby had told him she lived alone, so there was no danger of him being surprised by a housemate or a boyfriend.

Alex moved into the bathroom and filled the bath half full with warm water. He dragged Patty's body in and removed her clothes. Then he picked her up and lowered her into the bath, face down. Within ten seconds, she woke up and attempted to remove her head so she could breathe again, but he held the back of her skull with both hands to force her nose and mouth to remain below the waterline.

Patty flailed away for more than a minute before she gave up the fight, but there wasn't a moment when Alex relaxed his grip. He remained in position for another thirty seconds in case there was still some life left inside her, but there was only the quiet of her death to keep him company.

He twisted her body, so she was face up and manipulated her limbs to arrange them the way someone sitting in a tub might lie. Then he went to the kitchen and found two bottles of wine. He opened both and emptied one, throwing it straight into the trash. He only half-emptied the second and poured the red liquid into a glass. Alex placed the bottle and the glass on a ledge by the bath next to the tiled wall.

He collected Patty's clothes and took them into her bedroom. He hung up her blouse and skirt in the wardrobe and stuffed her underwear back in a set of drawers. Then Alex returned to the windowsill and examined the frame to see if he had made any scratches on the outside: nothing.

The stage was almost ready, she drowned in her bath after drinking too much. All Alex needed to do was to walk through each room and rearrange anything which looked like he might have touched it or that somehow indicated Patty had not been alone at the time of her death. He closed the kitchen/diner window from the inside and pulled the bathroom door ajar.

With a bit of luck, she wouldn't be missed until someone opened up the club after Kennedy's funeral. Even if a girlfriend were to come visiting, they'd have no reason to believe anything other than Patty was out when they popped over.

Alex listened at the front door: nothing. He poked his head out into the corridor and strained to hear any sounds from Patty's neighbors. Still silent. So he scurried down the stairs, out of the building, and off down the street to his car.

ANOTHER CIGARETTE AND Alex was ready to drive off, although his cuffs were still damp. He should have rolled his sleeves up a little more. Ten minutes of light traffic and Alex stopped around the corner from Fred's Bar on Elm.

He wasn't too concerned about Hank, but Amy had had plenty of time to see his face and remember it. She already knew he was a visitor to the area, and that was a little too much information for her to stay alive.

Alex entered the bar and took his seat at the back booth. Sure enough, within thirty seconds, Amy appeared to give him a menu and take a drink order.

"Just a coffee, thank you."

"Coming right up."

Most of the tables were occupied as though the death of Oswald had lifted a veil over the city. People were getting on with their lives and Fred's was a place worth frequenting.

Amy reappeared with a steaming mug of coffee.

"Cream?"

"No thanks."

"What can I get for you?"

"Steak and fries."

"How d'you want that cooked?"

"Medium-well."

"It'll be with you as soon as possible."

"No need to rush, Amy."

She smiled and switched off her waitress' expression.

"Hi, David. It's been so busy since they announced Oswald was shot on the television."

"That's fine. I'm glad that business is good for you."

"Are you going to be in the city for long? You said you were only here for a few days."

"I'll be in meetings until the weekend."

Amy smiled again as her eyes glanced over to an adjacent booth where a couple had just sat down.

"Go and work, Amy. You don't have to make small talk with me all afternoon."

She nodded and hopped over so that the man could ask for a pitcher of beer for the table. Fifteen minutes later, Alex's steak arrived. It was a bit too chewy, and the fries needed less salt, but overall he had eaten far worse in his time.

When Amy came to take his dessert order, Alex seized the opportunity.

"Any recommendations today?"

"The tiramisu is good if you have a sweet tooth."

"Then that's what I shall I have, Amy."

"Is there anything else I can get you, David?"

"There is one more thing, more a favor."

"Oh?"

"Would you mind if we had a… private conversation out back? There's something I'd like to ask you, but not here in the middle of the bar. Do you mind?"

She eyed him up and down and thought for a moment.

"I take a break in twenty minutes. I always have a smoke around then. If you are there when I am, then we'll talk and you can ask your favor."

ALEX TOOK HIS cue when Amy sashayed past him, down a corridor, and continued out the back of the building. Before the door had swung closed, he saw she had already lit her cigarette.

The rear entrance led out to two dumpsters, and some trucks parked fifty feet away. Amy sauntered toward them to escape the smell of the trash.

"Hey, you."

She leaned against the wall, one foot resting flat on the bricks.

"Hi, David."

Without her apron, Amy proved to have rather a slender figure beneath her white blouse and black pencil skirt. The blouse had Fred's logo on the chest. Alex lit a cigarette, shuffled uneasily, and smiled. He looked up at the sky.

"It's turned out to be quite nice, if you can forget the tragic events that have unfolded in the last couple of days."

Amy laughed.

"Yeah, the sun's out, David."

"Listen, Amy. I realize this is awkward, but you know that I'm only in town a short while and I was looking for some company this evening."

"Uh-huh."

"And I was wondering if you were free some point after your shift ends."

"Tell me, David. What do you have in mind for us?"

Alex worked hard to make his cheeks redden.

"Oh. I was thinking of a drink, or even a meal if you were up for it. Depends what time you get off, I suppose."

"You're a sweet guy, David, but I'm not too sure."

Alex stared at the ground as though embarrassed and disappointed.

"I understand. Why don't we both pretend that I am just not your type or too old and then my ego won't have to be any more bruised than it already is."

"Aw, shucks. Now you're going to make me feel bad."

"That was never my intention."

"A drink you say?"

"To get to know each other better. If we have fun, then that's a win. And if not, then we've had a pleasant drink and we go home… alone."

"What a gentleman."

"You know I tip well, Amy."

She laughed and finished her smoke.

"Tell you what, David. My shift ends at ten. If you are outside waiting for me, then we can try for that drink. If not, then all bets are off."

"You've got yourself a deal."

Alex leaned forward and pecked Amy on the cheek. She mumbled something about needing to get back and scurried into the building.

AT TEN ON the nail, Amy appeared from the front of Fred's and shouted goodnight to Hank. Alex stood outside and doffed his fedora at her.

"I'm glad you're here, David. I could do with letting my hair down and having some fun tonight."

She had changed out of her waitress uniform and wore an orange shirt and jeans, with a suede jacket on top, with lines of tassels running down the seams.

"Amy, are you into country and western, by any chance?"

"How d'you know?"

He flicked a tassel.

"Just call it a lucky guess. Where are we going?"

"There's a bar around the corner which serves a mean martini."

They walked east along the sidewalk and Alex worried Amy was taking them to the Carousel Club. One block down and they crossed the street to head north, so he relaxed. Up ahead was an alleyway, and Alex halted at its entrance.

"Amy, I know this is forward of me and we haven't even had a drink yet, but…"

He took her by the hand and walked them into the shadows of the alley, maintaining a gentle hold on Amy so that when he stopped, they stood next to each other. She inhaled as if to ask what he was doing and Alex put his first finger on his lips and then transferred it over to hers.

Amy placed an arm over his shoulder and leaned in toward him. She puckered up and closed her eyes. Alex grabbed her head and twisted it with all his force until he heard her neck crack. She fell to the floor and he dragged her corpse into the back reaches of the alley and hid the body under some boxes.

Then he hightailed it to his car and off to the airstrip. He only stopped to drop a dime at a phone kiosk.

"It's done."

"We figured as much."

"And I've made sure there are no loose ends."

Click. Whirr.

28

ESTHER COHEN CALLED her brother on the last day of the month. They spoke often as she and her nephews looked after Alex's interests on the East Coast. However, with his trip to Dallas making him impossible to contact, they had missed their November conversation.

"Alex, I've got bad news: we need you in New York tomorrow."

"What's happened?"

There was something about her tone to indicate this was not a business call.

"Mama fell yesterday trying to reach a top shelf of her kitchen cupboard. I don't know why she couldn't wait for one of us to pop over, but that's what she did. The doctor said she had broken her hip and left wrist, so we took her straight to hospital."

"Go on." His throat was dry, and a dull ache was emanating from the pit of his stomach.

"She rested overnight; that'd be last night. And David, Moishe, and I went over this morning to check on her. We were there for about an hour and she…"

The receiver was filled with Esther's sobbing, and Alex knew the rest. He inhaled and sighed.

"I'll get the first flight out today."

ALTHOUGH SARAH JOINED Alex for the funeral, she could not be next to him, as this was an Orthodox Jewish affair and the men and women stood in separate parts of the room. And as one of the official mourners, along with his siblings, Alex was positioned near the rabbi and close to the plain wooden coffin.

Even though they had arranged the funeral for the day after Ruth's death, the hall was packed with well-wishers. By the end of her life, Alex's mother had only a few friends who had survived the years, but word got out that respect needed to be shown to Alex's family member. If he had bothered to turn around, Alex would have seen some of the old Italian commission members, shuffling with ill-fitting skullcaps on their heads.

After the rabbi had muttered in Hebrew for far too long, the attendants followed the coffin to the graveside. Alex stood next to Esther and Aaron and Reuben, his estranged brothers, and in front of Moishe and David, and his three other sons: Asher, Elijah, and Arik. Again, Sarah was left to fend for herself in the main rabble. Alex clutched Esther's hand but wished Sarah was with him.

He had lived with death all his life, but at this moment Alex was crushed by the loss of his mama. He sniffed twice and cleared his throat. More Hebrew and as the oldest child, the rabbi pointed at a spade standing upright in the mound of earth which had been removed for the burial.

Alex plunged the blade deep into the soil and threw the contents on top of the coffin. As the dirt landed, there was a hollow thud as it hit the wood of the casket. He swallowed hard.

The rabbi leaned into him. "Not so much earth. You don't want to do yourself a mischief, and besides, there are plenty of people after you who must also take a turn."

Alex ensured the second pile still had some of the blade visible to lessen the load. The thud was just as hollow because this time the soil landed on a different part of the coffin. The noise pierced his heart again. For his third scoop, Alex did his best to aim the earth onto one of the two existing sprinkles of mud to reduce the agony of hearing it land, forcing the air to echo around his mother's body.

Then he planted the spade in the mound and moved a few steps away with Esther. His brothers were next, followed by the grandchildren. The rest shuffled back to the hall, but Alex remained by the grave, watching everyone who filed past and contributed to the burial of Ruth Cohen. By the time they reached the end of the line, he acknowledged Ezra and Massimo with a nod each. Then Joe Bananas, the boss of Manhattan, and Frank DeSimone from Los Angeles sidled by.

Alex was surprised to see Sam Giancana at the end of the line, the last member of the funeral party to contribute to the burial of the coffin. Before Alex walked away, from the corner of his eye, he noticed the cemetery workers finish the job off. As he reached the hall entrance, the rabbi stopped him for a second.

"We have had little opportunity to talk and there is one thing I need to know for the next part of the service: will you say Kaddish?"

Alex halted. The mourners' prayer?

"Can I read it please?"

The rabbi proffered him a prayer book, but it was all in Hebrew.

"I meant in English."

Rabbi Gould shook his head.

"It is only spoken in Hebrew."

"Then I decline. I only say things in a language I understand."

"If you think it's best."

Alex stared at Gould for a second and decided not to respond, grinding his molars instead.

ONCE THE SERVICE was over, the congregation formed a line after Alex and the other official mourners sat down in a row. One by one, people shook hands and wished them long life. Under Alex's instructions, Sarah didn't say a word and hugged him instead.

The Italian bosses made certain they were the last, so they could talk with Alex without halting the entire proceedings. Sam Giancana was the first to break the awkward silence.

"Alex, I speak for us all when I say I am so sorry for your loss. Nobody wants to reach the day when they must wish their parents a last goodbye."

"Thank you, Sam. She was a noble woman in her own way. She kept the family together when times were tough and was a rock onto which we all clung throughout our lives."

The men nodded and attempted to make small talk.

"I appreciate you taking the time out of your schedules to see me on this day."

"Alex, it is the very least we can do. But we do not want to intrude on your family's grief any more than we have to and shall take our leave of you now."

They shook hands and, for the first moment in all their dealings, each man gave Alex a firm hug and a pat on the back. Alex wiped a tear from his right eye and the bosses vanished from sight to be replaced by Sarah.

"Alex, we need to leave this place."

He looked past the woman with whom he had spent most of his adult life and realized they were alone.

"Hold me."

As Sarah took him in her arms, Alex cried. His shoulders shook up and down, and he could barely breathe. Once the wave of sadness had abated, Alex sat back down on one of the mourners' chairs and cried some more. Then he coughed and blew his nose.

"Let's get the hell out of here."

ESTHER HAD DONE a good job of preparing Mama's apartment for the funeral party. There were stacks of bridge rolls with a variety of toppings like chopped liver and smoked salmon. While her mother was not a big drinker, Esther had ensured she stocked the drinks cabinet well, with a large quantity of whiskey and vodka.

By the time Alex and Sarah arrived in their stretch limo, hired for each of the official mourners, the place was full of people. He hadn't been in the building since he walked out to join the army as a teenager. He shuddered as he entered the living room and those nearest turned round to check out the latest arrival.

Esther spotted them and dragged Alex over to Aaron and Reuben.

"A terrible reason, but this must be the first time in decades that all my brothers have gathered under the same roof with me."

His two brothers shuffled and mumbled something in such an incoherent way that Alex felt the need to be more forthright.

"Esther, it is a tragedy, but we are together again, right boys?"

"I never knew you had other siblings, Alex." He glared at Sarah for making the comment, but she was correct, he'd never mentioned them and, truth be told, it was a rare moment when he even thought about them. When he'd returned from France, they were still tied to their mother's apron strings and he was determined to make his way in the heady world of the Bowery. He didn't look back.

"My apologies, gentlemen. Let me introduce Sarah…"

"We heard all about her from Mama when you first walked out on us all." Reuben's eyes remained locked on the floor.

"Then when you moved away, she kept a scrapbook of your court appearances." That was Aaron's contribution to the conversation.

"It must have many empty pages. I haven't seen the inside of a courthouse since my federal tax problems."

"Alex, both Aaron and I stopped looking at that scrapbook after we left home. Mama still loved you even though you ignored both her and Pop."

"Given the circles I moved in, I thought it best if I didn't come round. Besides, I moved to the other side of the country."

"Whatever…"

The two brothers walked away, leaving Esther with Alex and Sarah, who squeezed his hand and pecked him on the cheek.

"They bear grudges, Alex, and Mama's death won't bring them near you soon."

"I know, Esther. Our paths diverged many years ago and we've led separate lives since. I don't blame them either. My life has not followed the straight and narrow."

At that point, Asher, Elijah, and Arik came up to their mother along with their spouses. They shook hands with Alex and engaged in polite chit-chat. It felt so strange to see his other boys. David and Moishe were part of his present and he'd lost contact with his other children before he moved to Vegas.

Later in the early evening, Alex and Sarah found themselves alone in a corner, the crowd having thinned out.

"Do you think I am still a member of this family, Sarah?"

"In a way, Alex. But the decisions you made all those years ago had consequences. By turning your back on these people to protect them from your business, you became disconnected from their lives."

"Does that make me an evil man?"

Before Sarah could respond, Rabbi Gould appeared, and Esther hurried to meet him and help him prepare for the evening prayers. She dragged Alex and the rest of her boys onto their rickety mourners' chairs and the service began as soon as they sat down. The rabbi didn't want to hang about.

While his siblings were going to sit the usual seven nights of shiva, Alex informed Esther that one night of praying was more than sufficient for him. So he and Sarah flew out to Las Vegas the following day to get away from everything.

29

AS EVER, TITO Vestri's limo collected them from the airport and deposited them outside the Emblem casino, owned by Ezra, Massimo, and Alex. Located just off the strip, tourists tended not to visit, but high rollers knew about it well enough to keep the roulette wheels spinning. Besides, the penthouse was fit for a president and several had been comped there over the years, including Jack.

Sarah insisted Alex stayed in their top-floor accommodation when they arrived.

"Let's at least take the rest of today to gather ourselves together. As soon as you leave this room, you'll throw yourself back into business, won't you?"

A shrug in response because she was right. Truth was that he had been expecting the call about his mother, maybe now, perhaps next year, but sooner rather than later. What he hadn't expected was the way his estranged brothers and children had treated him. Of course, they had no reason to behave in any other manner, but Alex hurt, nonetheless.

The following day, they ventured down to the restaurant for breakfast, where Ezra and Massimo were already sat at a table. They beckoned them over, and Alex and Sarah joined the lieutenants.

"We thought you would never leave your room."

"Ezra, sometimes even an old couple like us want to spend time together."

The corner of Massimo's mouth curled up and Alex scowled at him.

"I hope you appreciate the presidential suite."

"Massimo, of course."

Alex thought both men were behaving in an unusual way, but he couldn't tell if it was just the grief inside warping his perception. They settled down to breakfast and Alex ordered his usual feast, while Sarah took pancakes with maple syrup and a coffee.

"Careful you don't cut into our profits." Another jibe, this time from Ezra. What was their problem?

"If you are that concerned, then I'll just have coffee and toast."

"A mild roasting and nothing more, Alex. Go ahead. Enjoy. Massimo and I have business to look after, but we'll see you later."

After the men walked away, he leaned forward in his chair.

"Do you know what's got into those two, Sarah?"

"What do you mean?"

"I thought they were being snide."

"Alex, your mother died only a few days ago and you are not thinking at your best."

"I guess you're right… Do you see me as too old, Sarah?"

"What are you talking about, Alex? None of us are getting any younger."

"I know that. But sometimes I get so scared."

"This is the grief talking, Alex. Why don't you play some poker to pull your head back in the game? Meanwhile, I'll have a spa treatment."

THE ADVANTAGE OF staying in a casino you own is that there are chips to play with and a guaranteed seat at a table. Morning is always a quiet time with only nickel-and-dime tourists popping in after breakfast. As soon as Alex entered the room, the floor man pointed out a solitary table away from the entrance where a proper game was underway with three men and an empty chair.

"Do you mind if I join you guys?"

"It's a ten grand ante." The dealer's eyes remained fastened on the cards in his hand and on the green baize, so he failed to notice the owner of the joint stood in front of him.

"That's fine by me."

An hour later and Alex had acquired a pile more chips than when he'd arrived. He was about to cash out when the floor man tapped him on the shoulder and told him that Ezra wanted a private word.

"Alex, we thought we'd discover you in the gaming room. Remember that the house keeps ten percent."

"Ezra, if that is all we make, then you'd better find out who is skimming the take."

Laughs all round but Alex had a point.

"Anyway, what was so important that you needed to drag me away from my poker?"

Massimo eyed Ezra before answering. "We have a local difficulty, which we have tried to contain. We were hoping you could tear yourself from your game long enough to help us."

Alex smiled. Their attitude wasn't in his imagination.

"What's the problem?"

"Orazio Ferraro."

"That sounds like who. I asked what."

"He is a regular guest from Chicago; in here five or six times a year?"

Ezra nodded approval.

"He always pays his way and is a good tipper. Of course, his room and board are comped as the fella spends enough in the casino."

"Fabulous, Massimo. I'll be on my way."

"Alex, not so fast. When he came into town yesterday to play craps, we comped him ten thousand as usual, just as a token. He was on a losing streak and burned through the chips in a matter of minutes, so he demanded more on the house."

Alex blinked, knowing what was coming next.

"We declined but Ferraro insisted and we relented. He carried on that way all night. Then he left first thing this morning."

"And you allowed him to?"

"Alex, we couldn't think how to refuse the accommodation. He is the son of Frank Ferraro."

"Massimo, you would not have wanted to disrespect that fella in public. How much are we in for?"

"Half a million."

"Let me see what I can do."

ALEX KISSED SARAH goodbye for his overnight trip and grabbed a flight to Chicago that lunchtime. By the time he arrived at his hotel, it was five, so he ate a light dinner and headed straight to bed.

The next morning, he went to the South Side and found the area which Italians called home. All he needed to do was to go to a cafe and ask for Orazio, and everything else would follow. No sooner had he uttered the Ferraro name than the waiter fell silent, and the color left his cheeks.

"I don't know who you are talking about. I'll get your check."

The steward scampered back to the till and whispered something to the proprietor, who also immediately looked like he'd seen a ghost. Alex remained where he was, knowing that if he stirred his coffee for long enough then somebody would appear. And so it was. After the owner placed a phone call, a fella in a dark suit entered the establishment. A glance by the guy in Alex's direction and the man headed toward him.

"May I sit down?"

"Be my guest, if you tell me your name."

"Orazio Ferraro. I believe you were asking for me."

Alex beckoned Orazio to be seated with an open palm, indicating the chair next to his.

"Good morning, Orazio. Did you have an enjoyable time in Vegas?"

"Why, yes. How do you know that's where I've come from?"

"Orazio, I have business interests in the Emblem casino where you played."

"Great joint. My congratulations to you."

"The work is done by my partners, who inform me you have an outstanding bill to pay."

Orazio squinted as if trying to recall the name of a long-lost girlfriend.

"I don't think so. We are all square."

"Now this is when matters can get embarrassing for you, Orazio. While we comped your room, food, and drink, we are not in the habit of offering you more than ten large in complimentary chips."

"Do you know who I am?"

"Orazio, it is because I do that I am showing you the respect of coming direct to ask you for the half a million you owe."

"Go to hell. You walk into my restaurant and demand money from me? Get out now before we take you to the back and give your old hide the beating it deserves."

ALEX LEFT AFTER throwing a couple of bucks on the table to cover the cost of his coffee plus tip. Then he dropped a dime at a nearby phone kiosk and strolled around the corner and west two blocks.

The building was nothing to look at from the outside, and the signage indicated it was a private club for men of Italian descent. Alex was at the right place.

Frank Ferraro sat behind a large oak desk but walked around to shake Alex's hand. They sat down on armchairs at the other end of his office.

"Coffee, Alex?"

"Thank you, Frank. Sorry to bother you on such short notice."

"Not to worry, Alex. When you called a few minutes ago, I reckoned you would only do so if there was something important to discuss."

"That there is, Frank. And before we start, I want you to know that I come here offering you the utmost respect. Sam Giancana has only had exemplary things to report about you over the years, while you've been his underboss."

"Kind of you to say, Alex, but there's no need to blow smoke up my ass. How can I help?"

Alex sighed and lit a cigarette.

"A case of theft has come to my attention and I am seeking your assistance in resolving the matter."

"How much are we talking?"

"Half a million. Not a vast amount for men like ourselves, but neither is it chump change."

"Indeed. Who is the thief?"

Alex stared at Frank.

"Orazio, your son."

It was Frank's turn to sigh as he asked Alex to explain what his boy had done now.

"Alex, I apologize to you for my boy's foolishness and arrogance."

"No matter how hard we try, we cannot be responsible for our children's indiscretions."

"Tell me you have business in town other than this issue."

Alex shrugged.

"My mother died a few days ago, and I was taking some rest in Vegas when this situation arose."

Frank's cheeks flushed red and he gritted his teeth as he stormed out of his office. Much shouting ensued with the fellas in the anteroom, and Frank returned some five minutes later.

"Would you like another coffee or something to eat while we wait for my men to find Orazio?"

"He was in his cafe a short while ago."

"Alex, you have already seen him today, and he has refused to make restitution?"

"Yes, Frank. I respect you too much to have bothered you over Orazio's debt if I had not approached him first."

Frank nodded, and the two men waited, talking about old times, and sharing stories about Sam Giancana. The man might have significant interests in Florida, but he ruled Chicago nowadays. There was a buzz of muffled voices outside and Orazio entered the office.

The moment he did, both men stopped laughing and stared at him. Orazio's eyes widened as he recognized Alex from their earlier encounter.

"Boy, you have some explaining to do."

"What is he doing here?"

Orazio pointed a thumb at Alex, who returned the gesture with a smile.

"Alex has come to collect his debt and you are going to pay him."

"Why should I do that?"

"Because I am telling you to do so. Besides, this is Alex Cohen, a good fella who has worked with Sam Giancana more years than you have been on this earth."

Alex maintained his smile. This was just like the old days, and it felt wonderful.

JANUARY 1968

30

SARAH AND ALEX settled back into their comfortable life in Boyle Heights. He oversaw a sideline in narcotics, which remained focused on Hollywood, and Sarah ran the nafkas Alex procured for the stars and would-be celebrities. There were still his investments around the country and Alex had never given up his interests in Vegas and beyond. Each day began much the same as the last: with breakfast.

"Sarah, do you think we should retire?"

She laughed.

"Where did that thought come from?"

"I don't know. I'm wondering what's the purpose of dishing out pills and plants to the rich and famous in California."

"It keeps us in clover, doesn't it?"

"Sure, babe."

"Well then. Why change?"

Alex contemplated the question because Sarah had a point.

"I'm bored and want something else to do."

Another chuckle.

"Alex, if you are bored now, how do you think you'll feel after you stop working altogether?"

"I suppose…"

"You used to be involved in politics. Why don't you do some more of that?"

"Sarah, after the federal contracts from Jack Kennedy went away, I didn't have any leverage."

"Try state government instead then. We must have a senator or a governor you can bribe somewhere in this great state."

"Darling, I reach accommodations with people. I do not engage in mere bribery."

"Keep telling yourself that, Alex."

THE ECONOMIC BOOM had generated more construction work than anyone could have imagined. The trouble was that the Italians had got there years before. While he might have been late to the game, Alex had one card up his sleeve—his Hollywood connections.

"Thank you for seeing me, Carl."

"No worries. I am always happy to break bread with you. How's tricks?"

Alex and Carl Newman, head of United Studios, were enjoying lunch in Pietro's, an Italian restaurant on Sunset Boulevard.

"Carl, everything is just fine, thanks. How is the movie business?"

"You don't want to ask. The last couple of years have been very good to us, but right now we are stuck."

"What's the problem, Carl?"

"In a word, Alex, the Transport and Master Vehicular Workers. Nobody has got in or out of the studio in the past three days."

"What does the TMVW want?"

"Money, of course. What else does a union demand?"

"Better working conditions?"

"Funny, Alex. But this is serious. It's costing me tens of thousands every day the cameras aren't rolling."

"Perhaps I might intervene for you?"

"Is this your line of work?"

Alex chuckled.

"Like you have no idea, Carl."

"I'm sorry, Alex. Forgive me, but I've only known you as someone involved in… the party scene, shall we say?"

"One way or another, I have been a friend of the working man all my life."

"Alex, I don't give a damn about the working stiff. I care about my studio."

"Let me have a day to assess the situation. If I can assist, then I will be glad to do so."

"Alex, if you are able to sort this out, I'll pay your weight in gold."

"Be careful what you agree, Carl."

THE OFFICES OF the TMVW were like any other union place Alex had seen since his days in the Bowery. The first floor was filled with desperate men pleading with the receptionist for her to solve their problems. Meanwhile, the guys whose wages came from their dues sat upstairs with their feet on a desk doing nothing. So it had been, and so it was.

"Where do I go to speak to someone about the United Studios strike?"

"Listen, Mac. If you want to join the picket, just turn up and they will put you to good use."

"Miss, that's not what I meant. Who is responsible here for the action?"

"That'll be Emory Bourne."

"Where will I find him?"

"Third floor and follow your nose."

Alex tipped his fedora, wandered to the staircase, and heaved himself up the two flights. When he arrived at the landing, he took a breath and stared at the sign which listed office numbers and their occupants, but not in name order because that would have been too helpful. Instead, he stood and scanned the rooms to find Bourne's suite. No luck. A man hustled past in an open-neck shirt with hands in his pants pockets.

"Is Emory on this floor, bud?"

"Three eleven down this corridor, fifth on the right."

"Much obliged."

Before the passage took a left turn, room 311 was where the guy had predicted. Alex gave a quick rap and entered.

"Listen, bud, if you are here to support the strike, that's great but you've come to the wrong place."

Alex smiled and continued toward Emory's desk. Then he sat down in the only other chair in the office.

"Quite the contrary, Emory. I'm here to talk about ending the strike."

"Have I met you before? I know every studio hack Newman's employed and I've never seen you in my life."

"I am Alex Cohen and you are Emory Bourne. Now we both know each other's names, perhaps we could start talking business?"

"Get out of here. Who do you think I am?"

"Emory Bourne, I just told you."

Alex looked at this poor excuse of a man and waited for him to calm down and think straight.

"Are you from out of town and Newman has sent you over to strong-arm me and my boys into capitulating?"

"I live in Los Angeles and the only thing I wish to force on you is a conversation. Nothing more, nothing less. I am here to talk."

Emory leaned back in his leather seat, then sat forward to light a cigarette and inhaled his first drag.

"We have a list of demands. If Newman meets them, then we go back to work. And not a second earlier."

"Mr. Newman informed me the principal item of contention was money. I assume your brothers want more than the studio can afford."

"More than it is *prepared* to pay, Cohen."

"Call me Alex."

"Whatever. My men get up before dawn to pick up the stars from their mansions and wait around until they deign to leave late in the evening. Others spend their lives hauling equipment across country with impossible deadlines to meet. This is a strike about pay and conditions."

Alex smiled. "I told Carl this would be about more than just gelt."

Emory shifted in his chair.

"You said that to him?"

"Of course, Emory. This is not the first dispute I have worked to resolve and often both sides benefit because that way, everyone gains in the long term."

"You don't talk like a boss's lackey."

"I care about the working man. If he's not happy, then I'm not happy."

Emory nodded his consent at that thought, although Alex wasn't sure he knew what it meant.

"So, Emory, let's cut to the chase. We could spend hours in each other's company chewing the fat, but neither of us needs to do that. I expect what you want is to get a better deal signed and sealed before the end of the day. And I can deliver that to you, if you tell me what it will take to bring your men back to work."

"Improved pay and conditions. I've already told you."

"I am authorized to offer you a nickel on the dollar more in wages and one extra stop for drivers traveling over four hours."

"Not good enough, Alex."

"Emory, that is on the table. Five percent is generous and is more than Mr. Newman has offered until now. Let's face it, the two sides haven't even managed to be in the same room together. This is the first negotiation you've engaged in."

"We had months of discussions, Alex, but the studio would not budge an inch."

"That was when they thought they ruled the roost and that you wouldn't bite the hand that fed you. The TMVW has proved them wrong, but you and I need to work out a way to bring everybody together again. For the sake of your men and the rest of the hard-working crew who rely on the movies to put bread on their families' tables."

"Spare me the sob story. I know how important it is to have greenbacks."

"Emory, I do not doubt it. The funny thing is that when I first worked on union problems, I was young and naïve. I'd enter a man's office and offer some deal and if he refused, I would go to his home and threaten to kill his wife."

Emory leaned forward and the supercilious smirk left his face.

"But I am older and more worldly-wise than I was then. We both know that threatening a man with watching his wife's throat being slashed open by a stranger is an unnecessary experience. Are you married, Emory?"

A nod.

"Kids?"

"Two."

"Then you do not need to worry yourself. I will not go to where you live and terrorize your family. That is contemptible behavior."

Bourne leaned back in his chair. Alex leaped out of his seat and whipped around the desk so fast that the poor sap did not know what was happening. One hand grasped Bourne's throat and dragged him toward the window, Alex's other hand opened it up and he pushed Bourne out into the afternoon's air. A flash of memory of the night Alex killed Abe Reles, then snap, back into room 311.

"I've offered you five percent and an extra stopover. Accept that compromise or your kids won't have a dad."

"Don't…"

"Ketchup on the ground or a deal in your pocket. Decide now."

"HOW DID YOU get the job done so fast, Alex?"

"You were using the wrong kind of reason, Carl. Besides, I figured a small raise was nothing compared to the amount you've been losing every day."

"Let me show you some appreciation. Send me a bill for consulting services, let's call it one hundred thousand."

"Very kind, Carl. And thank you. To be honest, the original reason I wanted to talk to you was to find out if you had a private phone number for the governor. I know you two are close. You need to be, given how important Hollywood is to the state's economy."

"Sure thing, Alex. But I doubt if Reagan is going to be a politician you'll be able to do business with."

Carl wrote a different name and number on a scrap of paper from his pocket and passed it over to Alex.

"Much appreciated. And as you've offered me gelt, I'd be a fool to refuse the friendly gesture."

MAY 1968

31

THE NEXT DAY, Alex dialed the number Carl had given him and arranged a breakfast meeting with Driscoll Hart. As he drove into the Malibu Golf and Country Club, Alex wondered why Hart had picked this location. At the reception, a boy was sent to take him around to the clubhouse, where another man met Alex and walked him along oak-lined corridors, through the restaurant, and onto a patio area overlooking the golf course.

Hart sat nearest the golfing action, at a table with an enormous umbrella, so that Alex could only determine who it was when he was seated. To his surprise, Hart already had a guest who appeared to have almost finished her meal. Alex glanced at his watch and saw that it was only eight.

"Thank you for taking the time to see me, Mr. Hart."

"Call me Driscoll. There is no need for formalities, especially as you are a friend of Carl."

Alex eyed Driscoll's breakfast companion. She was only half his age.

"We haven't met, miss."

"Elizabeth was just leaving, weren't you, dear?"

She nodded, flicked her long blond hair behind her shoulders, and stood up. A kiss on the lips showed Driscoll and Elizabeth had not been engaged in a business encounter. And with a swish of her tail, she was gone. Driscoll's eyes lingered on her ass as she sashayed away.

"You must enjoy meeting your constituents. Or was that your wife?"

"My wife is at home and still asleep, but you didn't want to speak to me about my domestic arrangements."

A waiter arrived and took Alex's order.

"Over the years, I have built up a name in California."

"Mr. Cohen, you don't have to tell me about your reputation. It precedes you."

"Call me Alex. In that case, you are no doubt aware that I have been able to secure a variety of state contracts to the benefit of all those involved."

Driscoll took a slurp of coffee and swirled it around his mouth before swallowing.

"Alex, from what I've heard, you had some juice with Jack Kennedy and did business with Merrick Townsend. Jack is dead and Merrick has long since retired from politics."

"They are from the past, but I am interested in future opportunities, Driscoll. There is much we can do in this state to improve everybody's lives."

"Let me stop you there, Alex. The people of California elected me to do a job and I am here to serve them. I do not need you to come here and tell me how to work in the best interests of this great state."

"Driscoll, that was not what I was trying to say. My apologies if I have caused you any offense."

Alex's breakfast arrived, and the conversation paused while all the plates were delivered.

"Perhaps I was too circumspect. Are there any contracts I could bid for coming in the next few months, where we both could benefit?"

Driscoll smiled, revealing his perfect white teeth.

"I like a straight talker, Alex. There is always something we can work on together. The trick will be for us to find where our common interests lie."

◆ ◆ ◆

THEIR NEXT MEETING took place in the same Malibu golf club, although this time there was no sign of Elizabeth. Alex was hustled into a private dining room in which Driscoll sat alone. As a busboy cleared the table, it was obvious that the senator had eaten with two guests. And the fact they were no longer here indicated the politician was careful not to mix his associates.

"Would you like a drink, Alex?"

A Scotch on the rocks was ordered, along with a martini, straight up with a slice.

"I have been thinking about what you said, Alex, and there is a project coming up where we might work together."

"I'm all ears, Driscoll."

"The latest phase of the state water project has delivered vital water supplies to the San Joaquin Valley."

"I read about it in the newspaper."

"Right. So this means that the time is right for us to plan the next stage, which will go under the Tehachapi Mountains and send water to Southern California."

"You are talking about quite some tunnel, Driscoll."

"Tell me about it. There are a number of problems we face to push this through. First, the investment will be tremendous and we'll seek private funding. Second, the complexity of the engineering technology required to ensure that the water flows at a sufficient rate. Third, there is an environmental lobby concerned about the local wildlife."

"If you are thinking about asking me to bid for the construction job, then I can put a consortium together of like-minded entrepreneurs."

"Alex, no disrespect but if I am going to get into bed with the mob, the least I want is to sit in the same room as them when we iron out a deal."

"Do you think of me as a friend of the environment?"

Driscoll laughed.

"That's not quite where I have pigeonholed you, Alex. The way I see it is that I've heard you have a persuasive voice, shall we say, that might be useful to me when dealing with the lobbyists. To be honest,

I thought you would be more interested in funding the project. If only half of what I've heard about you is accurate, I reckon you could rustle up a billion or two without too much trouble."

"I know a couple of people. It is true."

"Alex, do not undersell yourself. You are a man of means in your own right, even before we consider how well connected you are with the wealthier element in our society."

Now it was Alex's turn to smile.

"And I assume you want to be seen to be out in front of this Tehachapi Mountains project before the Republicans jump up and down ahead of November's election. You're seeking a second term, I imagine."

"I serve at the pleasure of the people of California."

"Do you anticipate the vote will be tight? You won by only five thousand votes last time."

"Alex, if you'd encourage the unions to back me, then I would appreciate it. After all, the more secure my position, the easier we can get the Tehachapi Mountains project off the ground. Besides, it's good to work with friends."

They finished the last of their drinks, talking about nothing.

"Alex, as much as I'd like to spend the rest of the evening with you, I am expecting Elizabeth to arrive soon."

"Do you have rooms here?"

"There is a hotel as part of the complex."

"Does your wife know?"

"Yes, and she has accepted the situation. I look after all Mrs. Hart's financial, emotional, and physical needs. In return, she understands I will stay with her until the day I die only if I allow myself to spend time with women like Elizabeth."

"Been seeing her long?"

"Alex, your curiosity is getting the better of you. Let me answer the one question you are not prepared to ask. No, there is no opportunity for you to blackmail me over Elizabeth. If you attempted such a maneuver, then there are ways to silence you which would not involve a payoff."

He ignored Driscoll's attempt to threaten him.

"Driscoll, you misunderstood my motive for the inquiry. I supply many things in Hollywood and wondered if you needed anything for your recreational time with the young lady."

"HOW DO YOU feel getting into bed with Driscoll Hart?"

"Sarah, he lives under the same rock as any other politician I've met. He thinks he is different and implied he had some clout with the Italians, but deep down he is as self-serving as any other of those pond scum."

"Alex, remind me again what he wants you to do?

"Ballot stuffing for the November election and then fund a state water project worth a cool two billion."

"But rig the vote first?"

Alex grinned.

"You always have to do something for the cockroaches before they'll do anything in return, Sarah. And he'd like some coke for his girlfriend in the meantime."

"Some things never change."

"She's pretty, I'll give him that."

"Alex Cohen, are you getting ideas?"

"Don't get ahead of yourself, Sarah. I said she's cute, not that I'd want to do anything more than that. From the brief time I spent with her, I'm guessing that Hart isn't with her for the conversation. Besides, my days of two-timing you are long gone."

"Just you remember that. So are you going to put more effort into politics than the Hollywood party crowd?"

"I would like to, Sarah. At least it would be a great opportunity to move away from some of my illegitimate business interests."

"You raise one invoice as a consultant and you're going straight all of a sudden."

"Funny. But disentangling myself from the web I've created might not be such a bad idea. If I am heading to retirement, then taking income from a Californian water project is a better pension than siphoning gelt from the Emblem casino."

32

HART WAS ONLY one piece of the puzzle. For any of Alex's investments to obtain regulatory approval meant that his paperwork had to be in order, and that there would be no attempt to air his dirty laundry in public. He relied on David and Moishe to organize his documentation—they spent so much of their lives telling him to keep accurate records of legitimate business deals. Moishe almost fell off his chair when his father handed over his consulting invoice to Carl. "That's the first time you've ever bothered doing that. Congratulations, Pop."

To ensure his public house remained in good order required a fresh approach. Alex hadn't seen Bobby Kennedy since the night he'd introduced him to Marilyn Monroe. Those were far happier times for the country. Two assassinations later and the promise of the so-called swinging sixties had already been stolen away.

"Thank you for taking the time to see me, Bobby. It's been quite a while since we talked."

"Indeed."

Kennedy's campaign offices in New York showed the presidential candidate was not wanting for money. Alex wondered how much support came from the Italian American community.

"Congratulations on your win in Nebraska the other day."

"Thank you. My team worked hard and my message of peace and hope for the future resonated well with the voters."

"Your family has been successful at the ballot box."

"Alex, there is no need for you to drag my brother's memory into this conversation."

"He was a great man, Bobby."

"Jack lived among the greats and died as the greatest. But he is gone and I refuse to live under his shadow. I am my own man and create my own success."

"Sure, Bobby. I only meant that you were in good company. Nothing more than that."

Bobby glared at Alex as though he had slashed the face of Kennedy's mom.

"My mind is on Oregon now. That is one hard state to crack."

"If I can help in any way…"

"Alex, yours is not the support that my campaign needs or is seeking."

Those eyes bored through him. For someone who planned on becoming president, this Kennedy wasn't trying to win over every single voter.

"Bobby, I am surprised that you turn away help when it is offered to you. Your campaign funds must be fit to burst if you are prepared to refuse my money or more direct assistance."

"We might sit in New York but the days of Tammany Hall are long since over and you would do well to remember that before you offer me any inducements."

"You must think poorly of me, Bobby. You are accusing me of bribing you before I've made you an offer." Alex smiled. "Besides, those thoughts could not be further from my mind."

"I'm pleased to hear it."

"The actual reason I wanted to speak with you today was to talk about the California State Water Project. If Senator Hart is reelected, then he hopes to instigate a new phase of development. This would create blue-collar jobs in the state, especially outside Los Angeles."

"Increasing employment is something we can get behind. Rural areas need our support."

"I thought that was your position, Bobby. And how you would feel if I became the lead investor to the project?"

"Alex, I agreed to this meeting out of respect for my brother's memory. I understood you and he had a business relationship. Although I never inquired about that, I have assumed that it was not on the legitimate side of life."

Alex looked at the senator with a blank expression. There was nothing he wanted to say in response to the accusation.

"Bobby, whether or not you become president, I would still like your blessing on the state water project and my involvement. Are you able to give me it?"

"I could save you a lot of energy, Alex. Senator Hart is a good man overall, but he is a poor judge of character if he thinks he can rely on you as an investor in a major piece of state infrastructure."

"Bobby, I appreciate your honest and direct manner. While you may not believe me, I wish you well in your attempts to become president. My family tells me you have served as an effective senator for New York, especially in impoverished Brooklyn."

"Despite your sympathetic words, Alex, we both know that you and your kind are the enemy within."

"WHAT DID HE mean when he said that he thought my kind was the enemy, Sarah?"

"You were in the room. What did you think?"

"Jews."

Alex ground his back teeth and fumed for a moment. Of all the Kennedys, Bobby presented himself as the most liberal. As attorney general, he had put through several bills to give rights to minorities and the disadvantaged, and instigated projects to help the working man.

"Could he have been talking about the mob?"

"The Italians? They aren't my kind?"

"I didn't say the mafia, Alex. Organized crime, not just the commission."

Sarah asked a good question, and Alex had no viable answer. When Bobby had uttered the words, Alex found himself too shocked to respond and strode out of the office. Then he ruminated on the conversation for the entire flight back to LA and still wasn't satisfied by the time his plane landed.

Jack had been easy to read and easier to do business with. He enjoyed sleeping with sexy actresses and taking drugs while he partied. Whatever Alex may have thought about the guy, Jack never behaved like he was better than you. At least not morally.

He possessed what Alex now saw as a Kennedy superiority to the rest of the world, but when he talked to you, it was with respect. Bobby had none of that. He made a good political speech, but his disapproval spoke volumes when you were in the same room together.

Joe Kennedy, father of the clan, was a renowned anti-Semite, and the apple doesn't fall far from the tree— not this one, at any rate. But Bobby had worked hard to forge closer ties with Israel. Was that just because we needed influence somewhere in the Middle East?

The trouble with taking the high moral ground is that there is only one way to go, and that is down.

"If only I had something on him."

"You have the Monroe tapes, Alex."

"I do, but they don't prove he did anything, not even close. The most important tape comprises Marilyn calling him and Bobby not picking up. That is insufficient evidence to show he did for her that night."

"The senator is cleverer than Jack."

33

"I'M GLAD YOU are back in the land of the living, Alex. We haven't seen you since your poor mother passed away."

Sam Giancana sat opposite Alex in a small bodega in Cuernavaca, smack in the middle of Mexico. Two glasses of red wine stood in front of them.

"A lot has changed since we last saw each other, Sam." Alex gestured around the store, indicating how little the joint looked like Florida, where they had been meeting for at least the past decade.

"Alex, the cops wanted me to squeal, and that was not on the cards. To save myself the aggravation, I moved to this nonentity of a place."

"You think you'll get back to the US at some point?"

"Alex, Charlie Lucky always told me he was working on something, but that fella died in Italy, the land of his fathers. Who am I to make myself sound smarter than that great man?"

"But there's always hope and a talented lawyer, Sam."

"I'll drink to that."

They clinked glasses and continued to talk about the past; the days of Arnold Rothstein and Alfonse Capone.

"Thomas Dewey was a kitten compared to Bobby Kennedy, wouldn't you say, Alex?"

"Now that depends whether you were on the receiving end of his lawsuits."

"Alex, my apologies. I forgot he was the one who snared you for your taxes."

"Me and Alfonse both." Alex smiled and took a sip of his wine. Although he preferred Scotch, this tasted quite fruity and was more than pleasant, even if it hadn't come from a Californian vineyard.

"Why mention a Kennedy?"

"Alex, Bobby Kennedy will do whatever he can to prevent me from getting back to the States. That man might not be Sicilian but he knows the meaning of a vendetta."

"He swore me off a billion-dollar investment only a week ago. It was my opportunity to straighten my affairs so that my family would have a legitimate legacy and not be dragged into our world just to make a living for themselves."

"Bobby Kennedy is a cockroach. Do you have anything on him?"

"Only old recordings of him with Monroe. It's not enough to do him irrevocable harm, but it might help you if he tries to prevent your return to the US."

"I will bear them in mind. Right now, the Feds aren't out for me. I'm here in case they call another grand jury and try to drag me back to testify again. Mexico is a better option than jail. We both know that ratting out your friends is not what fellas do."

Alex nodded. His time in Sing Sing would have been cut short if he had sung like a canary, but he was no Abe Reles. Sam offered him a cigar, and he lit it.

"This is a mighty fine smoke. Local?"

"Cuban. I hope that doesn't leave a foul taste in your mouth."

"I got out with most of my money. Unlike Meyer."

"Alex, do you still believe that story he's been spinning since he landed back in Florida?"

"Sam, every time I've visited Meyer, he has been in this ordinary house and his fancy suits have long since vanished."

"That may be, but have you ever asked him how much the Lansky family is worth? I accept the man himself only has two cents to rub together, but that's because he put everything in his wife's and kids' names. The fella is a shrewd player."

Alex laughed.

"One of you is messing with my head and I can't decide which one it is."

"Alex, surely you don't believe Meyer has no income streams. You know how Vegas operates. Are you saying Meyer doesn't own a piece of at least one casino?" Sam chuckled and shook his head.

"But back to the matter at hand: Bobby Kennedy. What I wouldn't give to be rid of that guy."

ALEX MADE IT his mission to find Bobby on the campaign trail. He chased the man around Oregon until he landed the fish after a meet-and-greet in a diner in Klamath Falls.

"How's the presidential hopeful?"

"I'm surprised to see you again, Alex. I thought you'd turned tail and run away. Like a rat leaving a ship."

"Bobby, I've never been a rat. I honor my friends and am true to my word."

"Keep telling yourself that… I assume our meeting isn't a coincidence?"

"I was just passing through this nothing state and thought I'd drop by to see how you are getting on. I saw that McCarthy's claiming you made illegal recordings of Martin Luther King. Shame on you, Bobby."

Alex smiled at the same moment as Bobby scowled.

"Don't believe everything you read in the newspapers. When I was attorney general, I did whatever was within my powers to keep America safe from harm."

"Bugging King? Was he such a threat to the United States?"

"Alex, you are attempting to goad me and I will not fall for your ridiculous game. Now be off with you."

"Bobby, do you think I came all this way just to roast you? I need to ask you a serious political question."

"Spit it out."

"What is your position on crime going to be if you become president?"

"Alex, that is a stupid thing to ask. I will want to reduce it. There hasn't been a president in history who wanted to do otherwise."

"Bobby, perhaps I didn't make myself clear. When you were attorney general, you had a hard-on for organized crime. Won't you have more important matters to attend to if you move into the White House? I mean, we've got boys in Vietnam."

"A peace settlement will sort that out. And yes, I'd love to put an end to the pernicious effect the mafia has on our country."

34

ALEX MET SARAH in New York so they could spend a few days with their East Coast kin: Esther, David, and Moishe. The night they arrived, David held a large gathering of the extended family, including his wife and children. Moishe brought his girlfriend, having got divorced two years earlier, with nothing more to show for it than an alimony bill.

"Thank you for throwing this party, David."

"My pleasure, Pop. You remember Dorit, don't you?"

"Of course, although on this occasion we are experiencing happier times."

At that moment, Nathan and Jojo ran between the adults, almost knocking Alex over.

"Be careful with grandpa."

"Don't worry about me, Dorit. I used to have children of my own. Now they are all grown up, but they ran around at some point in the past."

Alex winked at David, who responded in kind.

"Sometimes I wonder if they'll ever calm down."

"Dorit, Jojo wants to be like her older brother, so when Nathan slows down, then so will she."

"That's going to be quite a few years into the future, Pop."

"I never said it would be easy, only that it will happen."

David nodded and Dorit scurried away to check on her darlings. She didn't have to search for long as both kids had zoomed straight for their Grandma Sarah. Alex surveyed the vista before him. The people he cared for all under one roof were a sight to behold and he smiled.

Sarah looked up at him from under a lapful of children and her eyes sparkled.

"It's a shame you don't visit them more often."

"You are right, Dorit. My work has taken me away from my family all my life."

"That's a good excuse, but some men would change their business if it meant they were closer to their families. They grow up so fast and there's only a short amount of time to enjoy their youth."

His daughter-in-law walked into the kitchen to prepare the next meal, leaving Alex to soak up the joy in the living room and to mull over what she had said. Soon, another son wandered over.

"How are you, Moishe?"

"Just fine, Pop. You and mom look well."

"We have no complaints. So tell me, who's that girl you're with?"

"Alecia Hefferman. From the neighborhood."

"And which area is that then?"

"She lives in Queens, but I met her in Soho."

"That's where you live, right?"

"Yes, Pop. We've been seeing each other for…" Moishe counted on his fingers. "…four months now."

"I'm glad you're keeping a tally."

"Your son is an accountant. What else am I going to do?"

"Does she make you happy?"

"Yeah, Pop."

"And can you imagine settling down with her?"

"Let's not get ahead of ourselves. We've only just started dating and neither of us knows how long it may last. To me, she's clever, funny, and makes me feel great about myself. What's not to like? But I'm a dull man and she is an attractive woman, and I understand how these things play out."

"Don't undersell yourself, my boy. You are an excellent catch."

"Now you're sounding like somebody from the old country, Pop."

"You know something, Moishe? Sometimes I feel I never left Broska."

"Is this my cue to maintain a fixed smile and nod when you tell me how tough it was growing up surrounded by Cossacks?"

"Not my plan, but I am happy to deliver if you want me to."

Moishe shook his head and moved back to Alecia, but Alex followed.

"Pleased to meet you, young lady. You must be Alecia. Moishe has told me all about you."

"Charmed, I'm sure."

She held out her hand and Alex shook the limp fish.

"It must be strange for you to be surrounded by someone else's family."

"I'm fine, thank you, Mr. Cohen."

"Call me Alex. There's no need to be formal around me. I am only his father."

Alex elbowed Moishe in the side, which made his son giggle for a few seconds. Alecia smiled.

"Sometimes they don't grow up much at all, Alecia."

She smiled again.

"When you don't tickle him, he behaves like a man most of the time."

"Will you two stop? I am standing right here in case you'd forgotten?"

"Son, we both see where you are. Now, do not be rude and interrupt the adults while they are talking." A wink in Alecia's direction.

"And are you working?"

"I'm in advertising."

"Sounds fascinating, but I must admit I have no clue what that means."

"Well, you watch television?"

"As little as possible, but I listen to the radio and read the newspaper every day."

"There you go. The adverts you hear and see don't just appear for no reason. The company I work for devises and makes the promo, then we place it in locations for the potential audience to receive it."

"Like on a billboard?"

"That's the idea."

Dorit came out of the kitchen and announced that dinner was served.

AFTER DORIT AND Alecia cleared the remnants off the table, they returned to the living room with Sarah and left the men to smoke cigars in the dining room. The two kids had long since gone to bed.

"I had an interesting conversation with your wife before we ate."

"How so, Pop?"

"She told me that a grandfather whose work prevented him from seeing his family would change his job to spend more time with them."

"I'm sorry."

"Don't be, David. There was no malice in her words, but her response made me wonder how much she knows of our business."

"That is simple. *Gornisht.* Nothing. I am a lawyer and I don't talk about confidential matters at home. She knows that I do some work for you, but she has no idea that you are my sole client or what that entails."

Alex took a sip of the Scotch that David had bought that week for his father to consume.

"And what about you, Moishe? Have you spun a story to Alecia about your work?"

"Not at all, Pop. I've told her the absolute truth."

Both Alex and David stared at him with jaws hitting the floor.

"I am an accountant and I look after your books. She asks no follow-up questions because in her mind the job is so dull in the first place that anything else she knows will make her fall asleep."

Big laughs all round.

"Are you concerned about a leak, Pop?"

"Not at all, David. I trust the pair of you and your judgment without any doubt. I got to pondering how well you have insulated ourselves from prying eyes."

"Moishe and I have learned from the best, Pop."

"Kind of you to say so, but you fellas must continue to be careful. I'm thinking of retiring soon and we don't want to slip up so close to the finishing line."

"You know that you've been threatening to stop work ever since I was old enough to walk?"

"This time I mean it, Moishe."

"No disrespect, Pop, but I'll believe it when I see it."

"MOISHE LAUGHED AT me tonight."

"Why would he do that, Alex?"

Sarah and Alex were in bed back at their hotel.

"I told him I was considering retiring."

Sarah giggled.

"I am not surprised you got that reaction. This isn't the first occasion you've made such an announcement."

"I'm serious this time, hon'."

"What makes this night different from all other nights?"

"Watching the family together this afternoon. How happy everybody appeared and the knowledge that I am missing out on seeing the grandkids grow up. Just like I did for my own boys."

"Alex, they only have their happiness because of the effort you put in to create the safety which they inhabit. David and Moishe earn a fantastic living because of your business interests. Don't sell yourself short. But the life you have chosen has consequences and there's no denying it."

Alex fell silent for a minute.

"How would you feel if we moved here, Sarah?"

"I prefer the Californian climate, but we might winter there and spend spring and summer here. Is this about coming back to your roots or to see Nathan and Jojo?"

"More the latter. When we left the Bowery, I turned my back on the place. If you recall, I only returned to resolve that unpleasantness with my mama's landlord."

"If we bought a house in the city, then you would need to stop working too. Not being in New York is just as absent from those kids as being on business, away in California."

"It's not where we live, is it?"

"No, Alex. You must face up to the consequences of the life you chose."

"Sarah, it's not only about what I want. You have a say in where we live and what we do."

"Is that true, Alex?"

"I believe so."

"Then when are you going to make an honest woman of me again?"

"You wish to get married to me? When last we spoke about this, you told me you never wanted that to happen as long as you lived."

"Alex, that was twenty or thirty years ago. You can't hold me to something I said when I was half my age."

35

AFTER TWO DAYS, Alex informed Sarah that he was going to have to leave.

"There's something I must do. And then I'll be back by your side and we need never work from that point on."

"How long will you be gone, Alex?"

"That's hard for me to say. A few weeks rather than days."

"You're not going to invade Cuba again?"

"Not this time. There are some matters I must straighten out and then we can live in peace."

"I know not to ask questions, but assure me that this is necessary. Whenever you are away, I worry whether you're coming back in a body bag."

"You and me both, Sarah."

"Don't joke. I would rather you carried on controlling Vegas and running nafkas and narcotics in Hollywood than be dead. There's no need to be a hero for the sake of your grandchildren."

"If we are to enjoy our retirement without interference from the Feds, or any other cops, then I must take care of one loose end."

ALEX FLEW OUT that night and landed in LA before taking a rental over to Berkeley. He might have looked more like a professor than a student, but he knew that if he waited long enough in that hotbed of political unrest, then he would catch the fish he wanted.

Each evening, he checked out society meetings and sauntered around the campus, searching for his quarry. Three fruitless days later and Alex found what he was looking for: a group of young Palestinians gathered by a monument facing Telegraph Avenue. It was only a couple of weeks before the anniversary of the start of the Six-Day War and emotions were running high.

"Zionist America needs to be stopped in its tracks."

"We can never be free in this, our adopted country until our brothers and sisters are free in Palestine."

"Israel must cease its oppression of the Palestinian people."

Alex held back that first time, observing and doing his best to melt into the background. From what members of the group were saying, it met every night at this monument and intended to carry on until their voices were heard.

The following day, he joined at the back again and one girl asked him what he was doing.

"I'm a visiting professor from NYU and would like to understand student grievances. My primary research interest is the mechanisms of political protest."

Rawda Qadir accepted Alex at face value and invited him to speak.

"As a mere onlooker, I do not think it appropriate for me to impose my thoughts on the group. All I ask is that you allow me to listen. Perhaps in the future, you will let me engage you in political discourse."

She nodded and huddled with some of her companions, speaking in a murmur, so Alex could not hear what was said. Every so often, one of them would look in his direction and then their head would bob down again and they resumed their private conversation.

By Friday, Rawda and her friends had accepted Alex and were comfortable talking in front of him about anything that popped into their minds. Most of the time, that was the state of the Palestinians in the Middle East.

"The last thing we need is for the US to prop up Israel with any more military support."

"Nothing is going to happen until January when the next president is sworn in. Do you think Lyndon Johnson will take any action before the election?"

Alex couldn't help himself. "And which candidate would you most like to win for the Palestinian cause?"

"Hubert Humphrey?"

"Why do you say that?"

"Well, no Republican is going to worry about the plight of a bunch of Arabs. And Kennedy is a Jew lover. That makes Humphrey the best of a bad bunch."

Alex nodded and pretended to write something down in a notebook he'd brought for that purpose.

"Anyone but Kennedy."

"Because?"

"If by any remote chance he gets elected, he has promised to send fifty jets over to Israel. None of the bombs on any of those flights will land on Jewish heads."

More fake note taking. The man who expressed this view differed from the others; he was the only one who was not a Berkeley student. The rest of them accepted him because of their commitment to equality and fraternity. Although nobody had mentioned his situation, Alex knew the guy was hopping from one short-term busboy job to the next, because Alex had already staked out his apartment and followed him over to that night's session.

"I WAS THINKING about what you said last night, Sirhan."

Alex pretended to bump into the boy an hour before the next meeting was due to start and offered to buy him a coffee in one of the many cheap cafes on Telegraph Avenue.

"What was that?"

"Of how you saw Kennedy as the worst option of all the presidential candidates. Do you think it'll make any difference to the Palestinians who is elected? Will US foreign policy shift that much if any of the mainstream candidates win?"

Sirhan Sirhan stirred his espresso for a minute.

"Perhaps you are right, George. The Americans will continue to support Israel, come what may, but that doesn't mean that some presidents won't be better than others. Those who are committed to the Jews will put more effort into propping up that regime and shall be less inclined to step in to protect my Palestinian brothers."

Alex nodded. "So what are the chances of Kennedy winning, of your fear becoming a reality?"

"George, if I knew, then I would also tell you everything else that is going to happen in the future."

They laughed, but the question had not gone away.

"Whatever else, that man is a Kennedy, so the mass media will follow him around like baying dogs. And the more he is seen and spouts his Jew-loving agenda, then he will sound strong and people shall be more inclined to vote for him."

Sirhan sipped his coffee and leaned back, satisfied with his response. If he skipped over the anti-Semitic details, Alex agreed. The more publicity the guy received, the more voters would be reminded that Jack's brother was on the ticket. And that was a mighty fine reason to put a cross in the box next to his name.

"Sirhan, what are you prepared to do to prevent Kennedy from becoming president?"

"That's an unusual question, George. You do not sound like a dispassionate academic observer."

"I am here for my university research, but that doesn't mean it is the only reason I came to Berkeley."

"No?"

"Do you believe it is an accident that I spend so much time with your group? There are so many activists at this school. What attracts me to yours?"

"I've not given it any thought, George."

"Well, have a think now."

Alex waited for Sirhan to consider the problem before him. Judging by his expression, there was much staring into the middle distance and few thoughts rattling around his head. After several minutes, he reached a conclusion. "You must care about the Palestinian cause."

"That's correct, Sirhan. And I would say I'm prepared to do more than talk about change. Around the world, students are getting off their asses and doing something for the values they hold dear."

"Like France, you mean?"

"Right. Are you willing to take direct action to protect your homeland?"

"What do you have in mind?"

"First, why don't you speak to the group and see if you can start leafleting the area. Not just students but reach out to residents."

"George, you think we should engage with the population?"

"There's nothing wrong with talk, but it won't save any lives. If there's anything I've learned in my studies, it's that change doesn't just happen. You have to forge it with your own two hands."

ONE WEEK LATER, Alex and Sirhan sat in the same cafe to review how their revolution was shaping up.

"It feels great to speak directly to people and let them know what is going on in the Middle East."

"Is that as much as you are prepared to do?"

"George, what are you asking?"

"How far are you prepared to go to stop Kennedy?"

"The group?"

"For what I have in mind, there isn't any need for everybody else to get involved."

"You're singling me out?"

"Let's just say that I have been watching you and believe you would be perfect for a special project. The question I have is whether you are ready to do more than hand out leaflets?"

"George, I am prepared to do whatever it takes to prevent that man from killing my people."

June 1968

36

THE AMBASSADOR HOTEL in Los Angeles was buzzing and had been all day. Alex and Sirhan were not surprised, as this was the makeshift Kennedy home, at least for a couple of days. The senator had toured South Dakota and California in the run-up to their two primaries and now that voting was nearing the end, the campaign settled into the Ambassador to wait for the results.

On the opposite side of the street to the hotel stood Protean Mansions, a residential block on Alexandria and Wilshire Boulevard. The hotel was set several hundred feet away from its main gates and offered some level of privacy to those who attended the various events that day.

Alex and Sirhan entered Protean with no difficulties. A quick trip around the rear of the building and Alex discovered a door to the backyard with an easy lock to pick. As soon as they were inside, they scurried up the stairs to the tenth floor and onto the roof.

"What next, George?"

Alex provided the answer without words. Instead, he unzipped one of his backpacks, which contained two smaller cases. He flipped open the first of them to reveal a firearm separated into several pieces, which he rebuilt as a rifle. Then he added the scope. He repeated the task with the second case and handed one of the firearms over to Sirhan.

"Now it's time for us to get used to the feel of our weapons."

The boy nodded and held the rifle like he knew what he was doing.

"Bullets, George?"

"Before we pour out the ammo, let's get into position and make sure we have a good enough view of the hotel. There's no point having slugs in the weapon and no way to hit our intended target."

Sirhan nodded again, and Alex walked him over to the right-hand corner of the building, facing the Ambassador. Once Sirhan had kneeled and looked through his scope to confirm he had sight of the Ambassador front, Alex jogged over to the left-hand side and hunkered down too.

Through his scope, he imagined moving from the gates, along the driveway, and a car halting outside the circular frontage. A sign announcing the hotel's name was set on the side of a dome, which pushed out from the main reception.

All of this was familiar because Alex had visited the Cocoanut Grove club on the hotel grounds many times before, often to see Frank Sinatra, Sammy Davis Jr., and the rest of their crew perform. The most important thing was that Alex would have a clear shot at anyone who was disgorged from their vehicle at the main entrance.

He checked his watch and saw they had ages before Kennedy was likely to show. He and his entourage wouldn't arrive until after the polls were closed. Even on election day, there was glad-handing to do. One thing he had learned over the years was that a sniper was never fresh if they'd been lying in wait for hours. He sauntered over to Sirhan and advised his mark to stand down.

"But I'm ready, George. Now is the time for action."

"We'll fight for Palestinian freedom when the sun sinks; that is when Kennedy will show and not before. You are going to get cramps if you sit there all afternoon."

"Should we go and come back?"

"No, Sirhan, let's stay where we are. The more time we spend away from this rooftop the more likely some concerned citizen may make us."

"I don't mind. If anyone sees me, I'll kill them."

"Now listen, Sirhan. We are here for a specific purpose and nothing should deviate us from that plan."

Sirhan looked down.

"And another thing is that not only do we want to get this job done, but we must perform it cleanly. There is no need to leave a trail for the cops to find us."

"There's nothing wrong with being a martyr, George."

"That might be part of your life plan, but it sure as hell isn't mine. I intend to execute the task at hand and walk away. You should aim to do the same. If you wish to carry on the good fight, then that is your decision, but don't jeopardize my ability to assassinate Kennedy and vanish into the shadows."

"George, if that is how you feel, then why do you want him dead? You've talked about the plight of the Palestinians, but your heart never puts fire into your words."

"Sirhan, I have my reasons and now is not the time for us to discuss them."

AN HOUR LATER, Alex passed a bottle of cola over to Sirhan, as well as something to eat. This was becoming a long afternoon and Alex wished he was alone. This felt nothing like any of his previous hits. No one was paying him for a start, but Sirhan was impatient and arrogant in equal measure.

"George, who do you think'll get the kill shot?"

"Does it matter? More important to remember is that we will be lucky to fire off a second bullet, so aim for the heart and not the head, unless he's walking away."

"We need him dead and not maimed, right?"

"If he survives the attack, then we'll have gifted him the election. Who wouldn't vote for an assassination survivor? Sirhan, make your shot count."

"George, he mustn't send those fighter planes over to Israel."

"That is what we are here to prevent. Now listen to me. Soon there'll be a slew of limos disgorging politicos, celebrities, and hotel guests out into the evening. The chances are that many of the men will wear a tux like Kennedy, so don't fire at the first person you see in a monkey suit. Make sure he is the right guy before plugging him."

"Have you done this sort of thing before?"

"That is irrelevant, Sirhan."

"You act as though you have."

"You believe what you want. I'm not answering foolish questions like that when we have business to take care of. The other factor that you must keep in the back of your mind is no matter what happens, if either of us is stopped or can't escape, then there was only one person on this roof. There is no need to kick off a manhunt if you are captured. Agreed?"

The boy nodded with eyes wide open.

"Speak to me, Sirhan."

"I agree, George. At least one of us must get away today so that others may know of the deeds we have performed."

"Don't go bragging. That's all I meant. And don't rat the other fella out. Nobody should conduct themselves like that. Now get ready."

Alex picked his path over the roof and back to his corner. Before getting into firing position, he looked over at Sirhan. The young man was poised, kneeling on the concrete with his rifle clasped in his hand. He might not be a Berkeley student, but he seemed to know his way around a firearm.

A quick look through his scope showed Alex that his prediction of a steady stream of vehicles was proved correct. Car after car disgorged men and women who waited a few seconds for everyone to leave the limos and then walked inside in groups, some in a hurry, others sauntering without an apparent care in the world. There wouldn't be much time between seeing Bobby and squeezing the trigger.

Another five minutes and the caravan of limos seemed to stretch forever. It had backed up onto Wilshire itself, despite the length of the driveway. This gave Alex a chance to survey the waiting vehicles before they vanished behind the hotel boundary walls.

The fourth limo from the gates. Alex was pretty sure he spotted Bobby's head in the back seat, along with a woman and two other men who he didn't recognize. A deep inhalation and he stared hard at that skull. It was still. Now was the time. As he exhaled, Alex's finger moved so that he felt how much pressure he needed to pull the trigger. Just as he was about to engage his muscle, there was a blur in the viewfinder, and the Kennedy vehicle lurched forward.

A deep breath and Alex tried again. This time there wasn't as good an angle, and he knew he'd blown his chance. Shooting at the man's nose would not kill him. Alex gave two short whistles and Sirhan repeated the noise in response, just as they had planned. Not long now and the limo would be at the front of the hotel.

One minute later, Alex had resumed his aim a little below the main signage. By now, the whole thing was illuminated and glowing off-white in the early evening breeze. Through the scope, he saw the woman from before exit the black limo and then two other men. This was it.

A lifetime later, Kennedy appeared and Alex placed the crosshairs in the center of the guy's head; the others who were milling around hid his torso, and he waited for Bobby to exit the vehicle. Inhalation and squeeze.

His bullet flew out of the rifle barrel and zoomed past Kennedy's ear. He must have felt the movement of the air because Alex thought he noticed the senator turn his head for a half-second before the slug buried itself in the soil of a nearby rockery. By the time Alex had steadied the firearm to take a second shot, Kennedy was nowhere to be seen. Alex stood up and hustled over to Sirhan.

"Any luck?"

"No, it all happened too fast, George."

"I got one shot off but was an inch too far to the right."

"What now?"

"We pack up our things and get closer to the man. This fight isn't over yet."

37

ALEX AND SIRHAN walked at a pace along the backstreets to Alex's car, which was parked in a lot some six blocks north. With the backpacks in the trunk, Alex pulled out a couple of revolvers from a sack wrapped inside the spare tire. He passed the first piece to Sirhan, who refused it.

"I already have one. I don't need another."

"Fine, but hide it in a pocket until we are ready. We must not get stopped by any cop for carrying a weapon, got it?"

They headed back toward the Ambassador to figure out what to do next. Alex used the time it took them to make this journey to figure out what they needed to do.

"Sirhan, we are going to walk straight in through the main entrance and join the crowd inside."

"What then, George?"

"We'll seize the moment. At some point, Kennedy will open himself up to our attack and then we shall pounce. You follow my lead and take my instruction."

They walked through the central gates, which created a gap in the boundary wall. Although he had arrived by car in the past, Alex knew his way along every twist and turn of the driveway. As they reached the entrance, the number of people surrounding them increased. Men and women spent most of their time talking about what they'd heard about how the vote was going. Alex stopped in the lobby and took stock.

The general flow was heading toward the main ballroom, and Alex was tempted to follow the majority into the rally. Then he remembered there was a bar on the first floor and took Sirhan there instead.

"Why are we here, George?"

"Because Kennedy won't show up on stage until he knows the results of today's vote, so we'll achieve nothing by standing around with the Democrat faithful."

They sat at a table near the back of the room and Alex asked for coffees for them both and a jug of water. The two men remained silent for a spell, even after the waitress had delivered their order.

"And now we wait, but at least this time we are seated in comfort and have a better sense of where the action is."

Alex nodded at one of the many televisions in the bar, positioned so that every customer could see a screen. Live coverage of the Democrat rally, along the corridor and off to the right, was beamed direct to their table.

"Do you have any idea what we are going to do, George?"

"Be patient. In every evening, there are highs and lows. It doesn't matter if Kennedy wins or loses tonight's races. At some point, he'll need to catch his breath and we will be standing by."

"I'd be much happier if we were doing something."

"We are. It's called waiting."

"You know what I mean."

"Have a sip of your coffee and if it makes you feel any better, have a stroll around the ballroom or see what is going on upstairs. Somewhere in this building are the key players in the Kennedy campaign. Just don't take any chances and try not to talk to anyone. When we walk out of here, nobody must be able to spot our faces in a line-up."

Sirhan smiled for the first time that day and took his leave of Alex. He came back thirty minutes later with a spring in his step.

"I think I might have an idea, George. The third floor is filled with campaign staff: if we wear a Democrat pin, then no one will give us a second look."

"And have you worked out in which room Kennedy is staying?"

"Not yet, but it seems like everybody is walking from one room to another. It is mayhem up there. Each time a statistic is announced on the television, everyone erupts in chatter and people scurry over to a different place to discuss tactics or something. I don't know what, but I covered most of the corridors and rooms without anyone stopping me and asking what I was up to."

"What are we waiting for?"

Alex threw some dollar bills on the table and followed Sirhan out of the bar and up a set of side stairs until they reached the third floor. Sirhan was right. Men and women ran down the corridors, popping heads into one area then another, many of them carrying clipboards and clinging to their pens like they would die without them.

They entered the second room on the left and Alex grabbed two clipboards, passing one of the treasured items over to Sirhan, then they headed into the next room along, where there was a flip chart but no television. The Democrats must have been using it as a store cupboard because there was every conceivable piece of stationery imaginable, including a cup of pens with a campaign slogan on the side.

"Take me to parts of the floor you weren't able to check out earlier."

Sirhan led Alex down the passageway, through a set of double doors, and into the continuation of the same corridor. Only it was much quieter here. The workrooms were near the lifts and stairs and none of the mayhem progressed beyond the doors they'd walked past.

Sirhan tapped Alex's arm and pointed to the far end then he leaned in and whispered, "Kennedy is here."

"How d'you know?"

"When I was up here earlier, I saw him vanish into one of these private rooms."

Alex chose not to ask why Sirhan hadn't bothered to follow the guy more closely. Instead, he focused on thinking about the next steps. The decision was taken out of his hands when a blond woman appeared from a room three along on the right. She held the door ajar. "I'll get those numbers for you, Mr. Kennedy."

Then she closed it behind her and walked toward the two men, who pretended to talk to each other and stare at their clipboards. They carried on with this charade until they heard the doors swing shut.

Alex padded down the corridor and stood with his back to the wall with Kennedy's door only three feet to his right. Sirhan was by his side, mimicking his stance. The thumping in his chest did not help Alex's concentration.

He had no notion how many were inside or if there were any cops in there with Bobby. So the idea of taking his chances and bursting in faded from his mind almost as soon as the notion had formed. No doubt, Sirhan would have considered that the best plan of the day.

At that moment, Ethel Kennedy appeared and Alex sauntered past the door to shoot a glance inside before continuing along the passageway to the end where he disappeared around the corner. Sirhan caught up with him and they waited until they heard Ethel walk down the corridor. Alex popped his head round to check on what was happening; she was gone but might be back any minute.

"I saw one Fed stood in the corner facing the door and picked out two voices other than Bobby's."

Sirhan nodded. Then his eyes widened. "You know Kennedy?"

"This is not the time for questions, my friend. If we kick down the door and go in shooting, the Fed will kill us before we've got into the room and fired a shot."

"Isn't it worth trying, anyway?"

An icy stare and a shake of the head.

"No, Sirhan, not now. This is not a genuine opportunity for us, even though it seemed it at first. If Kennedy was alone with his wife, then maybe I'd chance it. But I am not going face-to-face with a federal cop whose job it is to protect Kennedy from people like you and me."

As soon as those words had left Alex's lips, a roar and a cheer ripped along the corridor. Kennedy's door slammed open and Bobby scurried back toward the mayhem beyond the double doors.

"What was that, George?"

"I reckon Kennedy's just won a primary."

38

ALEX AND SIRHAN kept going, away from Kennedy's room, until they arrived at a stairwell. Back on the first floor, they vanished in the seething mass of people who were surging to the ballroom. Modern politics meant that Bobby Kennedy needed to be on television to celebrate his success and be seen to thank supporters for their effort over all these months. The speech wrote itself.

The two men went with the flow and joined Kennedy's acolytes to listen to the great man. Sure enough, he appeared on stage within ten minutes and droned on to the party faithful about their values and how this and that would be different. And he listened to the voice of the people. Yada yada.

While Sirhan's eyes were drawn to Kennedy, Alex focused on the different options for the senator to exit the stage. Bobby portrayed himself as one of the guys so much that he might try to walk through the crowd—there were enough eager hands to shake if he did.

But the place was packed to the rafters and it might take him a lifetime to get out. If Alex was in charge of Bobby's route, then he would take one of the side entrances and use service corridors. Everyone was so buoyant that Alex wouldn't have been surprised if they lifted the guy on their shoulders and carried him round the city like a king. A side entrance then, but left or right?

Alex's eyes switched from one side of the stage to the other, trying to guess which was more likely to be chosen. The patience he had warned Sirhan about earlier in the day bore fruit now. A busboy appeared on the right-hand side of the stage, which meant the kitchens were there, a perfect route for the senator to take after he stopped blowing smoke up his ass to please the crowd.

"Sirhan, pay attention to me. Work your way around the edge of the ballroom and aim for that service door." Alex pointed for a second and lowered his hand.

"On the other side will be the hotel kitchens. I want you to position yourself at a discreet distance and wait. If I'm right, then Kennedy will leave through that door and you'll be ready for him. Remember, aim for the heart and the head."

"Where will you be?"

"I'll follow behind him and be your wingman. Don't worry, I won't be far away."

Sirhan nodded and started inching his way through the mass of men and women gawping at Kennedy as he droned on. Alex counted to twenty and fought through the same crowd, but he took a different route, meandering through the people, but with the same service entrance as his goal.

All the while, he kept one eye on Sirhan, because he needed the boy to get there first. The last thing he wanted was for Kennedy to walk through those doors and see Alex standing there with a gun in his hand. A knife in the back was a different option, and there was a blade strapped to his ankle in case of need.

Fifteen long minutes later and Sirhan popped behind the door. Alex was ten feet away from the entrance himself and picked up speed to position himself against the wall, eight feet from the door.

"My thanks to all of you. Now it's on to Chicago, and let's win there."

A tumultuous thunder of applause and cheers erupted in the Ambassador ballroom as Kennedy waved to all parts of the auditorium and headed to the left. Alex ground his molars and considered taking a potshot at the guy there and then. That was the wrong direction. One of the entourage rushed out from the back of the stage and spoke with Kennedy, who nodded and turned round to go in the direction that Alex had predicted. He exhaled.

There were twenty feet between the bottom of the stage steps and the service door. The sheer number of people who wanted to congratulate the senator slowed him to a shuffle and Alex waited a full five minutes for one of Kennedy's handlers to open the door and let the man through.

Alex seized the opportunity and elbowed past everyone between him and that entrance so he could join Kennedy in the corridor before a security guard prevented the masses from following their leader into the kitchen.

KENNEDY AND TWO other men walked through an open kitchen area filled with stainless steel shelving stacked with canned goods. Bobby could only manage three paces before someone else stopped to shake his hand. Progress was slow and steady, but there was no sign of Sirhan. Perhaps he'd got scared and run away out the back or he'd chosen a hiding place so far from here that there was no guarantee of Kennedy reaching him at all.

The passageway narrowed and Alex sniffed an opportunity, so he increased speed to be only about an arm's length away from his target. He placed his hand on his gun, which was in his pants pocket. There was an industrial scale ice machine to the left and a steam table to the right. Bobby stopped for the umpteenth time to shake hands with a busboy.

A tray-stacker was positioned next to the ice machine. With no trays stowed, it looked like an empty metal carcass. Sirhan leaped out from its center and lunged toward Kennedy. One of the entourage was ahead of Bobby, clearing a path, and Sirhan brushed past him in his rush to get to the senator.

Sirhan raised his revolver and fired eight shots. As Sirhan began shooting, Alex dropped on his left knee and sent off five slugs toward Bobby. At least three went through the back of Kennedy's jacket, but Alex couldn't see if any had reached their target, despite being close enough to touch his ear. The candidate had taken a step or two back when Sirhan rushed at him.

In an instant, Kennedy dropped to the floor like a rock and Alex let others scoot past him. Under the cover of the fresh sea of bodies, Alex raised himself back on his feet to see a guy punch Sirhan in the face. He teetered but kept his balance in time for two guys to slam him against the steam table. Sirhan faced Alex's direction. His eyes were wide and wild.

He screamed and the two men let go for a second, giving Sirhan the chance to fire more shots, but he wasn't aiming at Kennedy, who was bleeding on the floor. Five people spurted red in front of Alex and Kennedy's guys grabbed at Sirhan and subdued him. This time, they had the smarts to take the gun off him and place it on the steam table, a big mistake, as Alex's accomplice was down but not out. Sirhan wrestled free once more, picked up the piece, and squeezed the trigger over and over, but there were no slugs left. This time Sirhan had no escape and Alex joined two other guys who pushed him onto the floor, face down, while what must have been hotel security cuffed him.

Alex had no chance to say even a word to Sirhan, but the fella blinked in such a way that he knew the guy wouldn't rat him out.

Then the flash of camera bulbs caused Alex to shut his eyes for a second. When he opened them again, the press hounds, who had been on the other side of the service door, had burst through and taken over the narrow aisle.

Alex knew there was nothing he could do for Sirhan and although he wasn't certain how many slugs had hit the senator, now was not the time to stop and ask questions of the witnesses.

He thought of pushing his way back to the service door but realized that would be swimming against the tide, so Alex moved forward along with the reporters, only he carried on past the subdued Sirhan and walked toward the kitchens.

People were rushing toward the senator from all directions, but most of the hotel staff had their work to do, so, within five minutes, Alex was in the back lot with a cigarette in his mouth.

Before the local police could swoop in and ask any unnecessary questions, Alex dashed south four blocks and then slowed down to a casual pace to take the three-smoke journey back to his car.

39

ALEX ARRIVED BACK home by three in the morning and woke up Sarah with a kiss on her forehead.

"Everyone is safe, but we need to pack a couple of bags and leave after breakfast."

They took turns behind the wheel for the drive to Florida. The plan was to aim for twelve hours traveling a day. As they pulled into the first of many motels on their route, the radio announced the death of Bobby Kennedy.

"Alex, how long do you think we will be away?"

"A week or two, Sarah. No longer than that. It's not like we're on the lam. I just would rather we weren't in Boyle Heights right now."

"Do you expect any uninvited visitors?"

"No, but that doesn't mean we shouldn't be cautious."

"Alex, you appear back home without me hearing a peep from you for three weeks and tell me to pack our bags as we're going on a trip. All that on the same day that Bobby Kennedy was shot. Now I love you and this is not the moment for me to ask you about your business, but I am not dumb either."

"Sarah, this is a precaution on my part and nothing more. There is nothing to connect me to Kennedy's death that I am aware of."

"And it is the things you don't know that make you want to leave town."

"We live together, we love together, but we die alone."

Sarah nodded and got out of the vehicle to pay for a night's accommodation. Alex hustled straight from the car and into their room once Sarah had the key.

"Are we going to be stuck in motel rooms from here to Miami?"

"Sarah, tonight is special, because I want to lie low. We've been driving all day and we are both tired. We'll only feel worse over the week. So let's crash out here where nobody will see us or care if we are passing through. Later, we can stay in some decent hotels. But not tonight."

She smiled and placed a hand on his arm.

"I'm glad you've tied up all the loose ends. That's what your absence was about, right?"

"Yes, Sarah. If we can ride the current storm, then everything should be peachy from now on. We must stomach some discomfort on this drive for the sake of our future."

THE REST OF the journey passed without incident and four days later, Mr. and Mrs. Bass checked into the Miami Colonnade Hotel, which overlooked the sea. The city had changed so much since their last trip, which had been several years before.

The same outré individuals still walked their poodles on the promenade that ran along the length of Collins Avenue by the Atlantic shore but with a difference. Martin Luther King and two Kennedys were dead. There was a sadness in the air, at least around any table where Alex and Sarah sat to watch the world pass by.

During the day, the couple stayed by the hotel pool rather than lie on the sandy beach as there were fewer people to recognize Alex within the confines of the Colonnade.

At night, they'd hit a local restaurant, but neither had the energy nor the inclination to visit a jazz club. So they would return to the hotel bar for a nightcap or two and retire to bed early. On the fourth day, Alex suggested they eat in the hotel and Sarah had no objection. The food was better than mediocre and the wine was decent.

"Sarah, have you enjoyed the last few days?"

"Miami has been fun but I could have done without the car journey. Next time, why not take a bus?"

Alex smiled while Sarah laughed. They both understood that they needed to leave the most obscure trail in their wake.

"Sarah, if we come back to Miami, I'll fly you by private jet."

"There is no point in showing off in front of me, Alex. Those days in the Bowery are long gone. You knew your tips meant I wouldn't need any other clients for the rest of the day. Back then, you were a mensch."

"And am I not one now?" Alex winked at her. Whatever moral ground he had stood on when he was a teenager, that mound had shifted, and he was down in the dirt with everybody else.

"Tell me, Sarah. What would you like more than anything in this world?"

"Apart from happiness, my children's success and untold wealth?"

"Put that to one side. Is there something you don't have that you wish you did?"

"Alex, why ask me what you already know?"

He reached out across the table and held her hand.

"Sarah, we have been together for a long time, decades, in fact. When we were young and wed, I caused you sadness and you have been kind enough to say that you forgive me for that. I am not sure I can ever forgive myself though."

She squeezed his hand.

"And when we were older and not married, we have told each other that we have found happiness in each other's arms. I know that is true for me. And you?"

She nodded and smiled.

"Sarah Fleischman, will you do me the honor of marrying me again?"

SARAH WANTED TO wait to tell the family in person, but Alex was desperate to share the good news with somebody. And Meyer was down the road.

"Hello, my friend. How are you?"

Meyer showed no emotion as he greeted Alex and invited him into his home. They hustled through and out onto the patio. Kids were playing in the pool.

"Meyer, have I called at a bad moment? There's no need for me to interrupt your family time."

Alex looked around to see Thelma and three middle-aged women, who he assumed were two daughters-in-law and Sandra, Meyer's only daughter. Their men must have been at work.

"Don't give it a moment's thought, Alex. They are here for the summer, so a few hours on one afternoon will not shake their world apart."

Alex smiled. Meyer had two marriages in the bag and three kids, and he took all of them for granted. To him, family was something that stayed at home while he went out and earned the gelt.

Thelma came over and offered the men an iced tea, which Alex declined and received his preferred Scotch instead.

"Alex, these are unusual times in which we live, wouldn't you say?"

"How so, Meyer?"

"Do me a favor. Don't act like you haven't read the papers. I'm talking about Kennedy, of course."

"Terrible business, Meyer."

"Depends whose business you own. On the television, they said the Arab killed him because of his attitude to Israel."

"Uh-huh."

"But you knew the Kennedys, both Jack and Bobby. What did you make of that?"

"The two men recognized the US needs a foothold in the Middle East. The Soviets have aligned themselves with the Arabs throughout the region."

"I met Joe Kennedy back in the day. I don't think I've met a bigger *verstinkener momzer* in my life."

"Meyer, I suppose you believe that the apple doesn't fall far from the tree?"

"Did it?"

"Jack was respectful of everybody. He was arrogant with everyone who he deemed inferior, but that was based on your station and not your religion."

"And Bobby?"

"Meyer, let's just say that Bobby and Jack were different people."

"That's what I heard. In that case, I'm glad he got his. Congratulations."

"What do you mean?"

"Alex, Bobby Kennedy gets assassinated and you turn up on my doorstep a few days later. Coincidence?"

"Meyer, I do not know what you are implying."

"I respect that you keep to the script, even with me."

They clinked glasses and Alex wondered how much Meyer knew and what was supposition.

"I thought you were retired, Meyer?"

"What are you talking about?"

"You said you heard talk about Bobby Kennedy. If you are no longer working, how come you are having conversations with men who are connected to the Kennedy clan?"

Meyer winked.

"There is not working and then there's retirement. I still maintain interests across this fine land and people are kind enough to visit me, like yourself."

"You've remained in Florida for a long time, Meyer."

"It's a safe state and there's a level of protection I receive in Miami-Dade that is not available elsewhere in the country."

"You remain with the Italians, Meyer?"

"Don't be ridiculous. I trust them about as far as I can spit, but there is an alignment of interests and as you know, that has always been good enough for me."

They sipped their drinks and watched the kids frolicking in the pool, enjoying their young lives without a care in the world.

"Is there any chance that you might make a trip to New York later in the year?"

"Now why would I want to do a foolish thing like that, Alex?"

"Because Sarah and I are inviting you to our wedding."

JULY 1968

40

ALEX SUGGESTED TO Sarah that he go alone to see Sam Giancana, but she didn't want to be away from him for that length of time. Not while he was concerned enough to hide out in Florida or beyond.

So he bought two bus tickets to Mexico City and from there, he paid near top dollar for a used car that took them further south to Cuernavaca. With Sarah secure in their hotel, Alex drove over to the cantina where he had arranged to meet Sam.

"I am pleased to see you safe and well, Alex."

"And this southern climate is treating you fine, Sam."

"It is still too hot and they do not know how to cook a decent bowl of pasta."

"This isn't Little Italy, but what is, right? I miss Lindy's cheesecake and no matter where I go, I can find no replacement."

"Alex, the world continues to spin on its axis and we must ensure we keep up. Times change, people change."

"The last time I went to Lindy's, they made me wait in line and wouldn't give me a booth at the back when it was my turn to be seated."

Sam grinned.

"If there's one thing I've learned, Alex, it's that you should never dwell in the past. The future is ours to shape."

"Wise words, Sam. With that in mind, I'm going to get married to Sarah."

"Congratulations, although I thought you were already hitched."

"We were, then we weren't. And now we'll jump the broom again."

"I wish you every happiness, Alex, but forgive me if I don't come in person, assuming you are planning on sending me an invitation."

"Of course, Sam. Given your circumstances, a telegram would be more than I'd expect that you do."

They sipped their drinks and spoke about nothing.

"It was a sorry business, Alex."

"What was that, Sam?"

"Do you not remember our conversation during your last visit?"

"We talked about many things."

"There is no need to play dumb with me, Alex. If Bobby Kennedy had won the Democratic nomination, we both know he would have gunned for organized crime. I would have been in his sights. So I thank you."

"Sam, there is no need to thank me, as I have done nothing. The senator is dead, and that is all."

"You are right to distance yourself from this sorry deed because as much as it gives me personal pleasure in seeing that mook buried in the ground, other members of the commission were unimpressed with your actions."

"I did nothing, Sam."

Giancana raised a finger to hush Alex's refutations.

"I will not insult you by pretending that you didn't pull off an amazing job. Respect to you and those who helped you. But you did not seek permission."

"From the commission?"

"That's right, Alex. This was not an approved hit and although the outcome benefits us all, you have angered some commission members."

"Let me get this straight, Sam. The biggest threat to the mob has been removed, but I didn't complete the paperwork right, and some bosses aren't happy because of this."

"Correct. So you and I must never meet again. The only reason you are not dead already is that I interceded on your behalf."

"What about my interests in Vegas and Atlantic City?"

"Make sure there is an intermediary between you and any fellas that you do business with. I am sure that is something you have had in place for many years anyway, but now is not the time to become careless."

Alex's stomach burned, and he grabbed his glass to get some moisture to the back of his throat.

"Then I must thank you, Sam."

"There is no need. You have improved my chances of being able to return to America without any grand jury demanding I rat out my friends."

Now it was Sam's turn to sip his drink.

"But as much as I like you, Alex, and the work we have done together over the years, I spoke for you out of respect for our mutual friend and business partner, Charlie Lucky. If it wasn't for him, then you would be dead. You should have asked permission first, Alex. They would have agreed to the hit on the turn of a dime. But you didn't ask, and that is not forgivable."

41

ALEX DUMPED THEIR jalopy as soon as they arrived back in Mexico City and Mr. and Mrs. Bass paid cash for their flights to the US. First, they went home and then they prepared themselves for a longer stay in New York.

David hosted the gathering again, with Esther, Moishe, and the wider members of the Cohen family. To save Dorit any effort, Alex hired caterers at short notice to supply food and drink, and he ensured his favorite cheesecake was on the menu.

They ate, they talked, they ate some more and then their waiters cleared the desserts from the table and Alex clinked his glass of Scotch with the back of a spoon.

"Thank you, everyone, for popping over today. Sarah and I know you had little time to get ready, but we wanted to share some news with you and sometimes these things are best done in person."

His sons nodded, as though they knew what he was about to reveal, and Esther stared agog at her brother.

"When we were here last, Dorit said something to me that put a fire in my belly. I couldn't shake it off."

David scowled at his wife, and she shrugged back at him.

"What did she say, Pop?"

"Moishe, I'm glad you ask and so I will tell you. Dorit challenged me about why I allowed my business activities to prevent me from spending more time with my grandchildren. It took a barrel of chutzpah to pose that question to me, but we all know her heart is in the right place and she is, above all, a *shayner maidel*."

Dorit's cheeks went bright red, and she pretended to blow her nose to hide her face from the world.

"So the first thing I have to tell you all is that we will leave Hollywood because three thousand miles is a very long way to schlep to see your family."

"Mazel tov."

There was a general murmur in the room, and then their sons came over and hugged both parents. When they had returned to their seats, Alex clinked his glass again to get silence.

"Of course, we all know that living on the other side of the country is just an excuse for not visiting; the plane journey takes no time at all. So there is a second thing I wish to tell you. I am going to make preparations so Sarah and I can retire. Living close and having the time will allow us to be with you. Like I should have been before now."

Alex took a sip of Scotch and watched all eyes stare at him until he placed the glass down again and carried on talking.

"And there's a third piece of news too that is as important to me as all that I've said so far."

With that, he sat down and nudged Sarah. She refused to stand but explained everything in a simple sentence. "We're getting married."

The room erupted with congratulations, hugs, and kisses as the extended family showed its approval. Moishe smiled. "I'm glad she's making an honest man of you after all this time."

AFTER A GOOD night's sleep Alex and Sarah sat in the Cohen offices, still in the Bowery. Everyone remained in high spirits and even Esther had broken out into a smile. Alex called them all to order for their shareholders' meeting.

"We need to plan how we are going to wind down my business affairs, especially those which have fallen outside of the federal tax regime."

"Well put, Pop." Moishe grinned.

"I have held conversations with certain people and while Sarah and I will quit our Hollywood activities, we cannot move to New York."

"Why, Pop?"

"David, you saw my business partners when we were in Havana. Let's just say that some of them have indicated that they not only expect me to wind down my operations but that I won't poke my nose anywhere near their businesses at any point in the future."

"So New York is no longer safe for you?"

"Correct, Moishe. I have worked hard to protect you from the details of my activities and that remains best for you all. If you become aware of what I do, and what I have done, then you and your loved ones will be under constant threat from now until the day they put a hit on you."

Alex stopped and allowed his words to sink in. As ever, David took everything his father said in his stride; he knew how to show a brave face to any situation. Moishe was more headstrong than his brother and prone to let his emotions shine through. He spoke first.

"So your retirement is our death sentence?"

"Not at all. Quite the reverse, in fact. You are all safe providing I retire. But Sarah and I cannot make a home in this state."

Esther chimed in: "Are you thinking of New Jersey?"

"No, and not Atlantic City before you suggest there."

Sarah laughed. "Chicago is out of the question too."

They all chuckled because they might not know the details of Alex's business life, but they read the newspapers and understood he was a gangster. Alex waited for everyone to settle down before continuing.

"Sarah and I had Florida in mind. The weather is good, there are beaches and the Italians might control Miami-Dade, but we would be under the protection of a reluctant patron."

"Is this just an elaborate ruse for you to live near your friend, Lansky?"

"Not quite, but he is about the only person left I know and trust outside of my family, Ezra and Massimo. Everyone else has either died a natural death or, more likely, been killed."

David had remained silent for a while, the finger of his right hand circling his chin and eyes half shut.

"You want us to move to Florida. This office, and our families as well?"

"Yes. There will be a lot less to do because we are only seeking to draw an income from our investments. Provided that money is safe, you fellas have my blessing to expand the legitimate empire as much as you see fit."

"How can I sell this to Dorit and the kids?"

"David, like I said yesterday, if they stay in New York, then I cannot guarantee their safety. If they are with you in Florida, they won't have a care in the world for the rest of their days."

"What about Alecia?"

"Moishe, if your relationship is firm enough, then she will come with you, and if not…" Sarah's words trailed away because she didn't want to disappoint her single son. This was the first woman he had connected with in years.

"And what about me?"

The timid voice of Alex's sister broke into the air. Alex smiled at Esther with a glint in his eye.

"We will always need you near us, sis'."

Sarah interjected. "If you like, we could buy a place with a guest cottage in the grounds so that you can have as much company as you want with us, but still get privacy when you need it."

"For real?"

Alex and Sarah nodded. They had discussed what to do with Esther early in their conversations about moving the family offices out of Manhattan.

"Unless there's any other business, I suggest we call this meeting to a halt and head out for a bite to eat. Anyone fancy a trip up to Lindy's?"

"One thing, Pop. What's going to happen to Massimo and Ezra?"

42

ALEX SAT IN Pietro's, the same Sunset Boulevard restaurant where he had met Carl. The food had been good and even though he wasn't a huge movie fan, he had to admit to himself that he got a buzz being near so many stars. The place was packed with people being seen to be there. Where else but in Hollywood?

He had placed his order for steak and fries two minutes before. When he looked up, he expected to see his waitress returning with his Scotch, but Frank Sinatra loomed above him instead.

"Good to see you, Alex."

"It's been a lifetime, Frank. How are you?"

"Not too bad. The great thing about singing and acting is that I have two careers. So if one is quiet then I've got something else to fall back on."

"If you have the time, join me, Frank."

Sinatra eyeballed the room and sat down.

"Concerned about being seen with me?"

A nervous smile rippled across Sinatra's face.

"Don't worry, I won't talk business to you."

"It's not that, Alex, but you know how this town operates."

"I do, which is why I'm going to be leaving it soon. I've been on the West Coast too long."

"Alex, you had a sideline in Hollywood parties. How will you run that if you aren't in the neighborhood?"

"My associates will take over from me. If any of your friends want to get high with a hooker, then they can still count on me."

They laughed and Alex's Scotch arrived.

"I should be going."

"Order something if you'd like, Frank."

Sinatra shrugged and perused a menu, settling on a steak too.

"Are you in touch with many of our Italian friends, Frank?"

"You know how it is. They never go away, and given the support they've shown me over the years, I am happy to do a few turns in Vegas to show my appreciation."

"We all grease the wheels to keep them running along the tracks."

"Right. For instance, I'm about to cut a deal to enable the sale of the Warner Brothers film studio, in return for relinquishing certain other assets."

"It is always the way, Frank."

"Here's a proposition for you. If you're not running whores anymore, why not take a job as a producer for me."

"Make films? You must be joking."

"Alex, if you can work for the mob, then you can assemble a film project. Think about it. You don't have to decide now."

"THANK YOU BOTH for flying over to meet with me here and not in Vegas."

Alex, Ezra, and Massimo sat in the Boyle Heights office with a mug each, poured from a large coffee pot the housekeeper had brought in from the other side of the pool. Alex thanked her and smiled to himself at the sight of the plate of cookies. "She bakes them herself."

"Maybe later, Alex. We are intrigued to find out what was so urgent."

"Ezra, even though it isn't anyone's birthday, I have a gift for each of you."

They looked around for a box covered in wrapping paper, but there was nothing to see.

"Ezra, I am giving you the narcotics distribution operation I have built up in Beverly Hills and Massimo, you shall have the Hollywood nafka network."

The two lieutenants glanced at each other before Massimo said what they were both thinking.

"Why, Alex?"

"I am exiting those businesses and as soon as I have extricated myself from all my illegal activities, Sarah and I will retire."

"You're kidding?"

"I have never been more serious in my life. Sam Giancana has made my position with the commission very clear to me. From this point on, I shall have no direct dealings with the Italians. No disrespect, Massimo. I mean, I can no longer do business with the mob."

Ezra whistled as he thought through the implication of Alex's words.

"Are you staying in Hollywood?"

"No, the plan is to relocate to Florida and take my family there too. This'll take time, but I intend to pass on or sell my assets as quickly as possible without creating a fire sale. The other issue is that we must manage this process as discreetly as we can, otherwise, some bosses will try to take advantage of the situation and move into our turf and take over our rackets."

Massimo cleared his throat.

"You said you will sell your assets?"

"Some of them, others not. I intend to gift you two most of my affairs, but there may be some elements that aren't worth hanging on to and I shall liquidate my holdings. After all, when I have to live on a fixed income, I want the cushion to be plumped up well."

"If you pass on any operations to us, then we will reach an accommodation with you."

"Ezra, you are kind to offer me restitution for my assets, but if I give them to you, then you must accept them with humility. Of course, I won't refuse any parting emolument, but to be clear, I am not demanding one. You fellas have built up these businesses ever since I visited Sing Sing and you deserve to reap what you have sown."

With their questions dried up, Alex led the men to the living room in the main house, where he poured three measures of Scotch.

"And by the way, Sarah and I are getting married again."

"It's been a long time coming. Congratulations."

"This calls for a toast."

"Quite right, Massimo. And I know what it should be."

"Go ahead, Ezra."

"To life. *Lechayim*."

THANK YOU FOR READING!

Get a free novella

Building a relationship with my readers is the very best thing about writing. I send weekly newsletters with details of new releases, special offers and other bits of news relating to my novels.

And if you sign up to the mailing list I'll send you a copy of the Alex Cohen prequel, The Broska Bruiser. Just go to www.leob.ws/signup and we'll take it from there.

Enjoy this book? You can make a difference

Reviews are the most powerful tools in my arsenal when it comes to getting attention for my books. Much as I'd like to, I don't have the financial muscle of a New York publisher. I can't take out full page ads or put posters on the subway. (Not yet, anyway).

But I do have something much more powerful and effective than that, and it's something that those publishers would kill to get their hands on.

A committed and loyal bunch of readers.

Honest reviews of my books help bring them to the attention of other readers.

If you've enjoyed this book I shall be very grateful if you would spend just five minutes leaving a review (it can be as short as you like) on the book's page. You can jump right to the page by clicking www.books2read.com/bilker.

Thank you very much.

Leo

SNEAK PREVIEW

In Book 7, The Mensch…

Alex Cohen stepped out of the shower and stared out of the bedroom window. All was quiet. The only discernible sounds were of his wife, Sarah rattling in the kitchen preparing breakfast. It had been a long few weeks and he was glad to be back home, safe in the knowledge that she was there for him, after all these years.

When he looked back on his life, he thought about the friends he had lost like Arnold Rothstein, Charlie Lucky and Alfonse Capone. The fellas from the days of Prohibition and the opportunities that sprang up around the country after the government bent to the people's will and allowed liquor back in the country. His mind rarely contemplated the hundreds he had killed: Abe Reles the Murder Corporation rat or Benny Siegel who had saved him when he'd left Sing Sing but had stolen money from the Italian mob. In fact, the only person whose death still haunted him was the sixteen-year-old who got a bullet between the eyes in the trenches of France during the Great War. And the army had given him a Purple Heart for that.

Alex got dressed and slipped downstairs into the kitchen. Sarah smiled at him and poured a mug of coffee and passed it to him.

"I thought it would be nice for us to eat on the patio this morning."

"Just like old times, Sarah."

He smiled and gave her a peck on the cheek, while making sure not to spill his coffee.

Alex looked up from his paper and pointed at the picture on the front page. "Have you seen this?"

The photo showed a stream of Vietnamese clambering up a ladder in the hope of escaping from Saigon in a US military helicopter.

Sarah's eyes glanced at the image, but she couldn't bring herself to look for too long.

"I can't imagine what it must have been like fighting in the jungles of Vietnam, Sarah."

"Does this bring it all back?"

Alex nodded and reached out to hold her hand. The Great War was civilized compared to what he had seen on the television the last few years. Everything had gone downhill since Kennedy was assassinated.

"Let's not dwell in the past, Alex. Just remember that we live together, we love together, but we die alone."

"I know. I guess I am sad that it has come to this." He flicked the newspaper. "America was supposed to be the land of milk and honey when we arrived at Ellis Island. Instead it has sent tens of thousands of boys off to be slaughtered and sent pictures home every night to show us what is being done in our name."

"Alex, you are almost sounding patriotic. I thought the perimeter of your concern was your family and your business interests."

"Most of the time, but now and again…"

Sarah allowed her husband to wallow in his thoughts for a few minutes and then she poured him another mugful. Then she lit a cigarette and passed it to him. Alex took three long drags and returned to the present. When he finished the smoke, he smiled and tucked into his breakfast: cereal, a bagel with smoked salmon, two cheese blintzes washed down with a large glass of orange juice, and coffee.

"Where's Veronica?"

Sarah laughed.

"We gave the housekeeper the day off, don't you remember?" Alex shook his head. "That way we could spend some time alone together."

A nod and Alex looked down into his lap.

"I have been a disappointment to you for so long, Sarah."

"Don't talk like that, Alex Cohen. Yes, you have made some mistakes along the way, but you have also done your best to be a good father to our children and be a provider to this family."

"Will you ever forgive me, Sarah?"

"I told you that I have done so already. If I had not, then you wouldn't be sat at this table. You'd still be back in Palm Springs. Let's not rehash old arguments. What's done is done and we have the rest of our lives to look forward to. Together."

"Thank you, Sarah."

"Just remember, Alex, that if you can't move past this then we will never be happy again. You must acknowledge what you have done to yourself and then accept the past for what it is. I know I am doing my best to, and you must do so too."

He nodded and stood up, gave her a kiss on the lips and mumbled about getting more of his affairs in order. Sarah remained on the patio and smoked a cigarette before taking the breakfast things into the kitchen and washing them up. Alex appeared from his office on the far side of the summerhouse, which was opposite the pool.

"I don't know what time I'll be home."

"That's fine. You'll be back as soon as you can."

"Do you have any plans, Sarah?"

"I might have a swim this morning and then visit the boys this afternoon."

"Twenty years ago, you told me off for still thinking of them as boys."

"That's right, but it is a mother's right to always think of her children as her babies."

Alex smiled, kissed her goodbye and walked out the front door. Sarah shuffled back onto the patio and slumped into one of the sunbeds. She shut her eyes for a second.

As soon as her eyelids were closed, the walls of the house shook and the windows rattled. A bang and the smell of burning metal and rubber. She ran to the front of the house: Alex's car was a fireball. Sarah slumped onto the grass and screamed.

To grab your copy, go to www.leob.ws/heel.

OTHER BOOKS BY THE AUTHOR

Alex Cohen

The Bowery Slugger (Book 1)
East Side Hustler (Book 2)
Midtown Huckster (Book 3)
Alex Cohen Books 1-3
Casino Chiseler (Book 4)
Cuban Heel (Book 5)
Hollywood Bilker (Book 6)
The Mensch (Book 7–Due Early 2022)
Alex Cohen Books 4-7 (Due 2022)

Jake Adkins PI

The Case
I Confess (Book 1–Due 2022)
Habeas Corpus (Book 2–Due 2022)
Luther's Diamond (Book 3–Due 2022)

The Lagotti Family

The Heist (Book 1)
The Getaway (Book 2)
Powder (Book 3)
Mama's Gone (Book 4)
The Lagotti Family Complete Collection (Books 1-4)

All books are available from www.leob.ws and major eBook and paperback sales platforms.

ABOUT THE AUTHOR

Leopold Borstinski is an independent author whose past careers have included financial journalism, business management of financial software companies, consulting and product sales and marketing, as well as teaching.

There is nothing he likes better so he does as much nothing as he possibly can. He has travelled extensively in Europe and the US and has visited Asia on several occasions. Leopold holds a Philosophy degree and tries not to drop it too often.

He lives near London and is married with one wife, one child and no pets.

Find out more at LeopoldBorstinski.com.